HER SISTERLY LOVE

A PRIDE & PREJUDICE VARIATION

LUCY MARIN

Edited by Jennifer Altman and Shari Ryan

Cover Design by Beetiful Book Covers

ISBN 978-1-956613-06-3 (ebook) and 978-1-956613-08-7 (paperback)

To my sisters-in-law

An excerpt from
Venta! within Thy Sacred Fane

But to her family alone
Her real & genuine worth was known:
Yes! They whose lot it was to prove
Her Sisterly, her Filial love,
They saw her ready still to share
The labours of domestic care
As if their prejudice to shame;
Who, jealous of fair female fame
Maintain, that literary taste
In woman's mind is much displaced;
Inflames their vanity and pride,
And draws from useful works aside.

— JAMES AUSTEN, 1817

ONE

Fitzwilliam Darcy could not account for his presence at a country assembly. He despised them, and this one looked to be the worst of any he had experienced. The rooms were shabby and the people hardly less so, in both manner and dress. But Bingley had insisted they attend, and Darcy was his guest; he could not refuse.

Mrs Hurst and Miss Bingley will complain about it endlessly for the next two days! Darcy suppressed a pained groan.

He was bored, and his mood was so sour he could taste it. People began gossiping about him as soon as he entered the room, he hated to dance, and he was never comfortable when surrounded by strangers. When Bingley had told him about leasing an estate and asked him to visit, Darcy had been pleased, even eager. His sister, Georgiana, was well on her way to recovering from a near-disaster the previous June and had gone to stay with their aunt and uncle in Worcestershire. That left Darcy free to spend the next two months however he liked. Bingley had talked about inviting a large party to Netherfield. The first blow to Darcy's spirits had come when, on the morning of their departure from town, Bingley confessed that the party would be only five: the two of them, Mr and Mrs Hurst, and Miss Bingley.

"I asked one or two others," Bingley had said, "but they were obliged elsewhere."

Darcy suspected they had had the good sense to avoid sharing a roof with Bingley's sisters and Hurst. *If only I had taken a blasted minute to think before agreeing to come!*

Bingley had continued, "We shall have a jolly good time in any case. Everyone I met when I was lately there was very friendly."

Very friendly, indeed, Darcy silently grumbled. *I have yet to meet one person here I would wish to befriend.*

He walked around the edge of the room, stopping now and again to watch the dancers. Whenever someone presumed to disturb his solitude, he moved to another spot. His shoes were new and the right one pinched his toes, yet he did not want to sit down. He had once, and an old woman had nattered in his ear for half an hour or more without seeming to understand that his silence meant he had no interest in talking to her.

Darcy had danced with Mrs Hurst, but he was avoiding asking Miss Bingley for as long as possible. Bingley intended to stand up with the beautiful blonde lady again—Miss Bennet. The set was about to begin when Bingley saw him, said something to his partner, and walked towards Darcy.

"Darcy, why are you skulking around in this stupid manner? You should dance."

"No, Bingley. You know how much I dislike it unless I know the lady. Leave me be and go enjoy your partner."

Bingley looked at Miss Bennet and sighed. "She is an angel, is she not? I have rarely seen such a beautiful face, and she is—"

"I am happy for you," Darcy interjected. He did not want to hear a lengthy soliloquy on the lady's character, especially since Bingley could know little about her.

"There are several ladies who are not engaged for this dance. Miss Elizabeth Bennet for one."

Darcy followed Bingley's eyes and looked at the young woman. He had noticed her before—while she danced with a youth whose face resembled a beet throughout the set or talked with her younger sister or Mrs Bennet. Although Darcy had been in the matron's presence for only a few minutes, it had been long enough to discover that she lacked decorum and was intent on thrusting her daughters into the arms of any marriageable man. Darcy was determined to avoid the lot of them and had not consented to an introduction.

"Return to your partner, Bingley. I can take care of myself."

Bingley shook his head and went away. Darcy's eyes drifted back to Miss Elizabeth Bennet. A young man approached her and her younger sister, whose name was Mary, he believed. Miss Elizabeth clasped her sister's hand and gave her what he imagined was a reassuring smile—it was difficult to judge with any accuracy at such a distance—and soon the man led Miss Mary away to join the lines of dancers.

Darcy moved closer to Miss Elizabeth, his gaze never leaving her. She watched Miss Mary dance, her expression almost maternal. After several minutes, Miss Elizabeth's gaze moved about the room until she found her eldest sister. Darcy was now close enough to see one of her eyebrows arch and the corners of her mouth twitch upwards. Next, she sought another—her mother, who was talking with Lady Lucas. Miss Elizabeth's expression turned into one of displeasure. She ran a hand across the back of her neck, then stepped towards the older ladies.

Darcy jerked his chin away. *What am I doing staring at her? Good God, what if someone noticed? If I am not careful, I will have a dozen of these people calling themselves my new best friend. She, like the rest of this company, will never be anything to me.*

ჩა

ELIZABETH WAS RELIEVED, but not surprised, to find that Mr Bennet had already retired by the time the ladies returned from the assembly. Whenever he shared a so-called joke about being disappointed that one of them had not eloped directly from the party so that he could begin to rid himself of his 'excessive' number of daughters, Elizabeth's stomach roiled. She was used to it, but Mary was not and the shock and pain on her countenance the first time she heard him make such a remark had left Elizabeth infuriated. Did he not care how his words affected them?

In addition, her mother was always full of either complaints or rejoicing after such events, depending on the presence of single gentlemen and how much attention her daughters, and she, had received. Her father would have anticipated Mrs Bennet being overly excited, and her effusions being grander than usual, thanks to Mr Bingley's presence. Indeed, Mrs Bennet had talked ceaselessly about how taken Mr Bingley was with Jane during the carriage ride home. After just a few hours, she was dreaming of what it would be like to have a rich son-in-law. Elizabeth's parents had already exchanged many harsh words about their new neighbour, to say nothing of their argument that morning; hearing Mrs Bennet's report on the assembly would likely have resulted in yet another quarrel. *But then everything that either one of them says or does is enough spark to set off a blaze, it seems.*

Elizabeth roughly pushed away a surge of resentment. While she was tired of needing to comfort her sisters during such interludes, it was a role she had assigned to herself, and as much as she wished her life could be different, she never regretted anything she did for her sisters.

Elizabeth had been twelve years old when she convinced Jane, twenty months her senior, that they had to do something about their younger sisters.

"You and I are old enough, and sensible enough, to fend for ourselves," Elizabeth had argued. "Mary, Kitty, and Lydia are not."

It was apparent to her that their parents' increasingly acrimonious relationship meant the couple's daughters were being neglected. It showed in their behaviour, and

Elizabeth had heard more than one person comment on Mary's increasingly sour demeanour and the lack of decorum displayed by Kitty and Lydia, who had also begun to taunt each other and their older sisters, sometimes using words similar to those their parents employed during their rows. She worried about what would happen to them if something were not done and did not trust either of her parents to rectify the situation.

What had finally prompted Elizabeth's actions had been a scene she witnessed just days earlier. Kitty and Lydia had been in the parlour with their mother, no doubt being fed more cake than was good for them. Elizabeth had been in the withdrawing room, playing the pianoforte. She was disturbed by her parents' voices, which were growing ever louder. Rushing to the room, Elizabeth flung open the door to see Kitty sitting on a stool, her shoulders slumped and eyes wide; Lydia had likely fled when the argument started. Mr and Mrs Bennet were on either side of her, not ten feet apart. Elizabeth's heart raced when she saw a candlestick in her mother's hand, her arm pulled back as though ready to launch it at her husband. It would not be the first time one or both of them had displayed their anger in such a manner. Flying to her sister, Elizabeth protected Kitty with her own body and was rewarded by taking the blow on her back that would have struck Kitty on the head. Despite her exclamation of pain, her parents did not stop, and Elizabeth quickly guided Kitty out of the room.

Mr Bennet retreated to his library for more of each day, and Mrs Bennet, who had never had a strong understanding, gave in to her nerves. Her chief activities became complaining—about her husband, the misery of her marriage, and her disappointment that not one of her girls was a son—gossiping, and spoiling Lydia.

"Such a pretty, lively little thing you are, my pet," Mrs Bennet said to Lydia again and again. "You remind me of myself as a girl. Oh, the gentlemen will go wild for you when you are just a few years older."

If Mr Bennet overheard a remark such as this, he would invariably respond by saying, "Then she can be another man's regret, just like her mother is mine." He would grumble about his ill fortune in having five daughters and had once told Elizabeth that, had she or Jane been a boy, he would have been spared the bother of having three additional children. They were at the breakfast table, and all of her sisters had overheard.

To Jane, Elizabeth had said, "Kitty and Lydia will end up just like Mama, and no one is paying any attention to Mary. You can see how much it hurts her, can you not?"

"What do you propose we do, Lizzy? We are not so much older than they are."

"I wish we had a governess," Elizabeth confessed. "Papa would say we could not afford it, and Mama would agree. I do not believe she sees the need for us to receive so orderly an education, and Papa would use it as an excuse to decrease her pin money, which she would find unacceptable. We shall have to fill the role and help our sisters learn what they need to know, even as we are learning it ourselves. We must be the ones to guide them, show them what it means to be proper young ladies. We can help them understand that...that this acrimony is not how a family should be."

Mr Bennet had claimed no interest in the matter when Elizabeth broached it with him, and, to her relief, Mrs Bennet had willingly, even eagerly, relinquished the task of instructing her daughters. It happened that they often did not see her all morning—unless the weather was poor and she required the company of one or more of them. Elizabeth supposed her mother was pleased to have the additional time to pursue her own pleasures; indeed, both of her parents were, in her estimation, selfish beings, and she vowed not to be like them and not to allow her sisters to be, either.

Elizabeth was pleased with the job she and Jane had done, although she knew it was not yet finished. Mary, Kitty, and Lydia were becoming rational, well-spoken young ladies who knew they were loved, and understood that there was greater value in peace and harmony than in the sort of relationship displayed by their parents.

What did it matter if Elizabeth had little time to indulge her own wishes—be they to take a long, solitary walk, experience the peace of being carefree, or read a particular book—as long as her sisters knew they were loved and were as happy as possible? What did it matter if she had to set aside her own pleasure at assemblies and parties in favour of watching over Jane and Mary and making sure her mother did not embarrass them too badly?

Elizabeth and Jane had long since re-arranged the bedchambers such that the two youngest could be each with an elder sister, while Mary had her own room. Kitty and Lydia were sitting on the bed in Jane and Kitty's room in their nightgowns, eager to hear everything about the assembly. Although it was the largest of the bedchambers the sisters used, it was crowded with all of them in it; but that, in its own way, made it cosy. Jane, Mary, and Elizabeth quickly changed out of their evening attire, and as the girls snuggled together, the three eldest told the two youngest about the evening. Kitty and Lydia were delighted to hear that Mr Bingley was handsome and amiable and that he had danced with all three of them, and Jane twice.

Lydia asked, "Who did he bring with him?"

Mary replied, "His two sisters, the husband of one, and his friend, Mr Darcy."

"What were his sisters like? Were they very elegant?" Kitty leant forward, her eyes alit with eagerness.

Jane's smile was one of happy remembrance. "They were, and they were so kind. Miss Bingley is to keep house for Mr Bingley, and she will be a wonderful neighbour and hostess."

Elizabeth had seen nothing to admire in either Miss Bingley or Mrs Hurst but held her tongue.

Lydia next enquired about the gentlemen.

Jane opened her mouth to reply, but then closed her lips and gently furrowed her brow. "I do not recall seeing much of Mr Hurst. He must have been in the card room for most of the night."

When she regarded Elizabeth and Mary to see if they had anything further to say about the man, they shook their heads.

"And Mr Darcy?" Lydia spoke quickly, her eyes wide and meeting each sister's in turn.

Elizabeth laughed merrily. "Mr Darcy would not talk to anyone beyond his own party, and he danced only with Mrs Hurst and Miss Bingley. He stalked around the room, his features puckered like he smelt something foul. I have never seen someone look more displeased to be in a place in my life. I agree that Mr Bingley was friendly and polite; Mr Darcy was not."

Almost before Elizabeth was finished talking, Lydia's next question was leaving her lips. "Is he rich?"

Mary nodded. "I heard he has ten thousand a year. Everyone was talking about it."

Lydia smiled mischievously. "That is very rich, indeed. I would put up with his surliness to have a husband with ten thousand a year! If I were two or three years older, I would make him fall in love with me."

Elizabeth bit her tongue to keep from snapping, *And end up like Mama and Papa? Mama flirted her way to a husband who was a good catch. We live with the result of their carelessness in choosing a marriage partner.* But Lydia was young and immature, and Kitty was little better. To Elizabeth, they exemplified why young ladies should be kept at home until they were seventeen or eighteen.

She met Jane's eye and sent her a silent request to say something to correct their youngest sister. Her voice calm and gentle, Jane said, "Respectable men want more than a wife who knows how to flirt, Lydia. We should all remember that if we want to make good matches."

Elizabeth nodded. "We must show ourselves as women worthy of being esteemed. We do that through our behaviour—our sense, intelligence, kindness to others. We may not end up with husbands who have ten thousand a year, but we will have husbands who treat us well and the comfort of happy lives."

Lydia twisted her mouth into reluctant agreement and nodded. Jane embraced her.

To all of her sisters, Elizabeth said, "It may not be right to think this way, but to get away from Longbourn, our only hope is through marriage. I pray that each of you meets a man who can give you the love and care, and good home, I know you deserve."

"You do, too, Lizzy," Jane said.

Elizabeth smiled and wrapped an arm around Mary's shoulders; they rested their heads against each other.

Jane said, "I believe you wanted to know about the assembly. Emma Goulding wore a new gown."

The sisters spent the next half an hour discussing what their neighbours wore and who stood up with whom before saying their good nights. After they climbed into the bed they shared, Elizabeth told Lydia how proud she was of her, especially for working so hard on her French lessons, which Elizabeth knew she hated, before they drifted off to sleep.

TWO

The next morning, Elizabeth arose at her customary early hour and slipped out of the house. It was a pleasant autumn day. Although the sky was mostly overcast, it was not particularly cold or damp. She walked along the banks of a stream, listening to the water trickling over rocks and branches, the faint smell of rotting leaves in her nostrils. She thought about the assembly and smiled at the recollection of dancing with several agreeable gentlemen and sharing a laugh with Charlotte Lucas. Remembering Mary and how she had held her own made Elizabeth's heart swell with pride. She was so thankful that Mary had been able to put off going into society until she was eighteen, and Elizabeth intended for Kitty and Lydia to do likewise.

Elizabeth and Jane had both been brought out far too young. Elizabeth had known it at the time, but she had been powerless to prevent it. Mrs Bennet had been eager to show off her most beautiful daughter and had insisted Jane come out when she was sixteen. Jane had been nervous about the prospect and, with Elizabeth's assistance, had managed to put off her mother's demands for the better part of a year. At that time, rather than allow Jane to wait longer, Mrs Bennet had decided that Elizabeth, although only just turned fifteen, would also have her come out to keep Jane company. While Elizabeth liked to meet new people and expected it to be exciting to attend parties and balls, she had known that neither of them were yet prepared for so momentous a change in their lives. Elizabeth had tried to get Mr Bennet to intercede on their behalf, but he would not.

Elizabeth had quickly grown to dislike the attention some of the older gentlemen paid her and discovered that it was too easy to be flattered by the flirting of the younger gentlemen. After just two months, she was on the verge of being desperately in love with the son of a neighbour—until he lured her into a dark corner during a card party and tried to kiss her. She punched him in the ribs to escape his embrace.

As for Jane... A sudden light-headedness made Elizabeth reach for the support of a nearby elm. Jane had almost been ruined. *My mother was too busy gossiping to notice what was happening with her daughters. Especially that night—* She pressed a hand to her temple, her head reacting violently to the memory. Jane, Elizabeth, and Mrs Bennet had attended an assembly. Mrs Bennet had been with several older ladies, her voice carrying across the room as she complained about Mr Bennet and how much she would have preferred to have a son rather than any of her three middle children. She had been saying the same things to different ladies, and several gentlemen, all evening, having found a particularly willing audience. Gone was any notion that she should be chaperoning her daughters—not that Elizabeth had ever supposed she took that duty to heart. Elizabeth had grown anxious when she could not find Jane. When she had gone looking for her, she had found her and Mr Chaplin in an unused room, Mr Chaplin's hands where they had no business being, and Jane's gown askew. Even now, Elizabeth did not know how Jane had lost all sense of propriety. Elizabeth had fought the young man who had tried to tempt her; Jane had succumbed. Again and again, Elizabeth thanked God that she had found her sister when she did and had managed to extract her from the situation without anyone learning of it.

Jane was left heartbroken and mortified. Perhaps Mama did see what was happening and simply did not care? It is possible. If anyone discovered the truth, Jane would have been forced to marry—if Mr Chaplin could have been convinced to do the honourable thing. It would have given Mama something to crow about for years to have a daughter married so young.

Elizabeth did not blame Jane for the affair. To be sure, she was too willing to think the best of people— which worried Elizabeth—but at the time, she had been so young, which must excuse her poor judgment.

Elizabeth did not know what made her think of that horrible time this morning, and she shook her head to banish the memory to history. She and Jane had learnt from the experience and could avoid similar missteps in the future—and prevent their sisters from falling prey to unscrupulous men. Even though they did not talk about it, Elizabeth was certain that, like her, Jane understood that they could not be too careful when it came to men they had lately met and about whom they knew so little, no matter how amiable they seemed. Mr Bingley was the latest example of such a man. They did not even know family or friends who could speak on his behalf and assure them that he was an honourable gentleman.

Wealthy men, those from the ton, *come to the country to amuse themselves with sport and perhaps a little bit of flirtation. They are not interested in falling in love, especially not with young ladies without dowries or connexions. Jane may have been flattered by his attentions at the assembly, but she would not be so foolish as to believe it meant anything more than that he appreciated her beauty.*

Taking deep lungfuls of the fresh, clean air, she allowed the quiet and peacefulness to restore her spirits. All would be well.

§&

UPON HER RETURN to the house, Mr Bennet summoned Elizabeth into his library. She sat in a wing chair whose arm had been unevenly patched, the wide expanse of his walnut desk between them. He tossed a piece of paper across the table in her direction.

"Tell me what you make of that."

Elizabeth placed her bonnet and gloves on the side table next to her before standing and retrieving what turned out to be a letter. As she read it, she pulled her eyebrows together. It was two full pages of the most flowery prose she had ever had the misfortune to read. It took her a moment to recognise the name at the end; it was from Mr Collins, who was her father's heir.

When Mr Bennet prompted her to reply, she said, "Well, it is...surprising. In more ways than one. I gather this is the first you have heard from him?"

He nodded. "It is an absurd letter. What a manner of writing he has! At once a mixture of pomposity and humility. Could he not simply say that he has taken orders, has a living in Kent—he makes his patroness sound like a saint—and would like to heal the breach in the family?" With a snigger, he continued, "Do you not feel kindly towards him, Lizzy? His apology for being next in line in the entail and the injury it will do to you and your sisters was very handsome, and he wrote that he wished to make you amends."

Elizabeth rolled her eyes. "As if he could avoid being your heir or could make us the only amends that would matter and allow one of us to inherit in his stead. It hardly seems the letter of a sensible man."

Her father laughed. "Oh, I have no expectation of finding him sensible at all. He might be prevailed upon to marry one of you, however, for which I would thank him."

Elizabeth ignored the last part of his remark. "What will you do?"

"I suppose I must respond. You noticed that he proposed visiting next month?"

She nodded.

"He would be an amusing guest, but I have no stomach for a visit at the moment. I shall put him off. Perhaps in the spring or next summer."

How like him to ignore what he finds disagreeable. Mr

Collins may be a fool, but he will inherit this estate; for the good of those dependent on it—including my mother and sisters— Papa ought to do more!

Mr Bennet reached for his book and muttered, "Well, off with you."

❧

AS DARCY HAD EXPECTED, Bingley's sisters spent the day after the assembly complaining about everything from the drive to it, the people, the musicians, even the colour of the walls. Bingley insisted that he was excessively pleased with his new neighbours. Hurst cared nothing about it as long as his glass and plate were full and his days were spent at sport and cards.

Darcy's opinion was closer to that of Mrs Hurst and Miss Bingley, although he kept it to himself. While he was used to much finer, the rooms et cetera did not bother him so much. But the people! He hated to be the object of attention, especially when that interest was centred on his wealth. As though he were nothing more than his income!

Worst of all was Mrs Bennet. Bingley was full of praise for the eldest Miss Bennet, and Darcy agreed that she was very pretty. Mrs Hurst and Miss Bingley called her a sweet girl, which was quite a concession from two who were more likely to find fault with others, especially young unmarried ladies.

She could have been the most beautiful and kindest lady in the country, and have the largest fortune and best of connexions, and I still would avoid her. Who would want to associate themselves with a woman like Mrs Bennet?

Darcy admitted to himself alone that—for some indiscernible reason—his gaze had been drawn to Miss Elizabeth Bennet more than once, but it meant nothing. He simply found her manner...uncommon. She seemed particularly attentive to what her sisters and mother were doing, whereas he would expect any young lady to spend an assembly searching for dance partners and attempting to attract eligible gentlemen.

The Netherfield party met the Bennet ladies at a dinner party several days after the assembly. Once arrived at the Stuarts', Darcy had greeted Miss Elizabeth and her mother and sisters politely enough and then slipped away. Mrs Bennet had immediately latched on to Bingley, and Darcy refused to be trapped into a conversation he knew would be at best uncomfortable, but more likely inane. He watched from across the room as Bingley stood with Mrs and Miss Bennet, his eyes wide open, as Mrs Bennet blathered on about who knew what, one hand clutching her daughter's arm. Miss Elizabeth had clasped Miss Bennet's hand for a moment before taking Miss Mary over to talk to Miss Lucas.

Good God, stop it, man! Darcy reprimanded himself when he realised he was, once again, studying Miss Elizabeth. *Someone will notice and leap to the conclusion that I am interested in her. I am not. Her behaviour is unusual, and in such tedious company, it is enough to draw my attention.*

At dinner, Miss Elizabeth sat almost directly across from him. Darcy sat between Lady Lucas, who was more interested in speaking to the man at her other side, for which he was thankful—Lady Lucas was little better than Mrs Bennet—and one of the Miss Gouldings, who, as he had expected, had nothing to say for herself.

Miss Elizabeth, however... She wore a soft ivory gown with deep blue ribbons that somehow brought out the richness of her skin and hair. Her long neck was exposed, and Darcy imagined her skin was warm and soft. While observing her as she talked to her companions, he discovered two things. First, her attention again moved between her two sisters and mother. Second, she appeared to be intelligent and well-informed. She spent the better part of the meal explaining to Sir William why some scheme related to the waterworks in Meryton was a good idea, adeptly bringing him around to her point of view while using such an artless, playful manner that the older man no doubt believed he had always been in favour of the notion.

Darcy was discomposed to find that it took a great deal of effort to avoid her company after dinner. He *wanted* to go to her, to learn more about her and discover what sort of young lady she was, why she was always so vigilant when it came to her family, and what she thought about books and art and the benefits of the country versus town. Instead, he contented himself with observation; if he watched her, overheard more of her conversations, his curiosity would be satisfied without any possibility that someone would notice and think it meant more than that he was bored and had no other way to occupy himself.

By the time Darcy returned to Netherfield that evening, his urge to know more about Miss Elizabeth Bennet had taken root in his gut, whether he was willing to admit it or not.

OVER THE COURSE of two dinner parties, one of which was at Longbourn, an outing to see an ancient cathedral and Roman ruins in a nearby town, and a card party, Elizabeth had a chance to observe Mr Bingley and his guests. It was evident to Elizabeth that Jane very much liked Mr Bingley, but Elizabeth knew better than to trust his intentions. She liked Mr Bingley, who appeared to be a friendly, amusing man, but he was young—not even five and twenty—and had taken a short lease on an estate in order to enjoy the pleasures of the country for a few months. She expected he would be gone by the end of the year, and she could not bear the idea that Jane would be injured by him.

During a moment alone one morning, while Mary was helping their younger sisters practise their drawing, Elizabeth said to Jane, "I think Mr Bingley is amiable, but do be cautious. It is evident that your regard for him is growing, but you hardly know him. You must be on your guard."

"He is just what a young man ought to be, Lizzy. He is kind and attentive, and I enjoy speaking to him. Very much."

"You forgot to add that he is handsome," Elizabeth said. "I know you favour blond gentlemen."

Jane blushed and pinched Elizabeth's arm. "Tease! As if I would choose any friend simply because I liked to look at them. Think nothing more about it. You worry too much."

"You do not worry enough." Elizabeth linked her arm with Jane's as they strolled in the garden. She spoke lightly so that she did not sound like she was reprimanding her sister. "People will talk. You know our neighbours have already heard Mama speculate about you and Mr Bingley. How can you judge his character after a few hours spent together here and there?"

"What harm do you think he can do me?"

Elizabeth stopped walking, and Jane followed suit, removing her arm from Elizabeth's and looking at her. There was something about Mr Bingley that reminded Elizabeth of Mr Chaplin, whom she had initially liked but whom she had grown to despise. *Perhaps it is more Jane's immediate infatuation with him than any actual resemblance between the two men.* Whatever it was, it left her very uneasy. She had no wish to remind Jane of her past errors, but if Jane did not think of it, she was likely to make the same mistake again.

"If he, if both of you, continue on as you have been acting, people will begin to expect an engagement. Then, when he leaves or makes it plain that he has no serious intentions towards you, you will be left with a broken heart and a damaged reputation."

Jane's cheeks became as red as ripe strawberries. "Perhaps he will prove honourable."

"Jane..."

"I *like* him, Lizzy, and I like his sisters. You think too meanly of the world."

Elizabeth bit her lips together for a moment, as if trying to keep the words from escaping. They would not be held back, however. "Mr Chaplin. If I had not been watching, if I did not find you when I did—"

"I was not yet seventeen!" Jane cried. "I made a mistake. I admit it. Must you remind me again and again?"

Elizabeth had not alluded to the affair in years. "I

have no wish to distress you, Jane, only to keep you from—"

"Give me credit for being wiser now. Besides, Mr Bingley and I have only known each other a fortnight. No one is thinking about marriage."

"Our mother is," Elizabeth replied, thinking that she would have believed her sister more had Jane been able to meet her eye. "Mr Bingley is charming and handsome; any lady would mistake his amiability for something more. I must mention his sisters. Be careful with them."

Mrs Hurst's and Miss Bingley's preference for Jane would seem to indicate good taste, but Elizabeth did not believe they were genuine. She saw the sisters exchange too many looks that suggested they liked the neighbourhood no more than Mr Darcy did, and she had witnessed them rolling their eyes or hiding mocking smiles behind fans more than once.

Jane, her colour high and eyes bright with tears, refused to look at her.

"I only want to see you—and Mary, Kitty, and Lydia—safe and happy." Elizabeth gently caressed her sister's arm.

"Let me judge what will make me happy. You must trust me."

Elizabeth forced her doubts into submission and smiled. "I do, Jane, of course I do." Her sister was older now, as she had said, and would not be as incautious as she had been during that earlier affair. *I must not drive her away by arguing with her. There is enough conflict in this house as it is. I will…observe her and Mr Bingley. Just to be sure.*

The sound of Mrs Bennet's shrill voice calling their

names ended their conversation, and they returned to the house.

As she sat in the withdrawing room with her mother and sisters, Elizabeth resumed her contemplation of the Netherfield party. She had yet to find anything to admire in Mr Darcy, apart from his good looks. He rarely spoke to anyone other than his friends, and soon people stopped trying to engage him in conversation. She did not understand how someone could remain so aloof or why they bothered to be amongst those they clearly despised.

To Elizabeth's amusement, it was soon evident that Miss Bingley had matrimonial ambitions when it came to Mr Darcy. The gentleman did not appear to return her interest.

But I do not know him. For all I know, it is already a settled thing between them, and his bored, almost annoyed demeanour is a way to hide the deepest love. Elizabeth chuckled to herself. *I would not like such a betrothed, but he is rich, and many ladies would tolerate a great deal from a gentleman in Mr Darcy's position if only he promised to make them his wife.*

THREE

At the start of November, Elizabeth attended a party at Lucas Lodge with Jane, Mary, and her mother. There would be card tables for anyone who wished to play, music, perhaps a little bit of dancing, and certainly a great deal of conversation and food. The entire Netherfield party was in attendance, and Jane was soon chatting with Mr Bingley; Elizabeth cared not what his companions were doing.

The chief excitement for the first hour was the news that an encampment of the militia would be stationed in Meryton for the winter. Several gentlemen had already met some of the officers and eagerly shared their impressions. More soldiers would be arriving in the coming days.

Later that evening, Elizabeth found herself standing with Charlotte Lucas. They spoke about the party for a few minutes before a comfortable silence fell. It was broken by Charlotte.

"Mr Bingley is quite taken with Jane. I am happy for her, but she is too reserved. If she wants to secure him, she must do more to show that she welcomes his attentions, to flatter his feelings to greater heights and encourage him to come to the point as soon as possible."

This was the sort of talk Elizabeth had feared would arise. "Charlotte, they hardly know each other. Pray do not fill Jane's head with such notions." *Or anyone else's. The Bennets are gossiped about enough as it is.*

"I do not agree. They are both young and unmarried, and it is natural to speculate about them making a match of it. Any couple can be happy or miserable together, Lizzy. It is a matter of them deciding which to be and making it so. I would rather any husband than facing the future I see before me. Always a burden, no value unless I undertake those disagreeable chores my brother's wife—when he has one—does not want to do, never the mistress of my own home, never a mother. Yes, I say a thousand times, Jane should secure Mr Bingley as quickly as possible."

Mrs Long joined them, and, while Charlotte listened to the lady tell a rambling story, Elizabeth's thoughts wandered. She felt a surge of sympathy for her friend. At twenty-seven, Charlotte felt the danger of her age. At twenty, Elizabeth was in no such peril, but she also knew she would likely find herself in a similar situation to Charlotte's in a few years. Elizabeth had decided long ago that she could not leave Longbourn until her sisters were married and settled in their own homes. She could not recall exactly when she had made the vow. It might have been the morning Kitty was almost injured, or perhaps the first time she heard the unmistakable sound of flesh striking flesh. Fortunately, her parents' arguments seldom descended to those depths, although her father or her mother would have an obvious bruise or other injury now and again. Elizabeth had done her best to shield the younger girls from the worst of Mr and Mrs Bennet's behaviour, but as they had grown older, it had become impossible.

An episode just that morning underscored the detestable nature of their home life. She recalled the harsh sounds of her father's voice which carried up the stairs and through the door of Jane and Kitty's bedchamber where the Bennet sisters had gathered to weather the storm. While Jane comforted Kitty, Elizabeth had stood between where Mary and Lydia sat, one hand clasped in Mary's and the other on Lydia's shoulder.

"Because I told you not to, you stupid woman!"

Mrs Bennet's shrill voice made it difficult to make out exactly what she said, despite the loudness, and Elizabeth could not tell what the argument was about—money, their dissatisfaction with how the other behaved, or likely nothing in particular.

"You may regret me all you like, madam. I assure you; I regret being married to the silliest, most ignorant woman in the county!"

The sound of Mr Bennet's last words was so loud that Elizabeth supposed he had moved from the parlour into the corridor. A few seconds later, a door slammed shut forcefully enough to make half the house shake. Mrs Bennet's wail then filled the house as she called for Hill.

An hour later, they were all going about their days, acting as if nothing untoward had happened.

Elizabeth's heart raced, and she bit the inside of her cheek to force her mind to the present. Mrs Long and Charlotte were now talking about the weather and Mrs Long's certainty that there would be an inordinate amount of snow that winter.

As much as she tried to prevent it, Elizabeth soon slipped back into her private thoughts. She knew Mr and Mrs Bennet's interminable bickering affected each of her sisters deeply. Jane grew quiet and simply endured the interludes, giving her attention to whichever sister most needed comforting. In between arguments, Jane, with her need to see only good in the world, preferred to pretend everything was well and refused to speak about their situation, even to Elizabeth. Mary was stoic, holding herself too tightly; she had once dug her nails into her palms so much that she left a mark. More and more, she said only what she must to her mother and father, and Elizabeth worried that she was becoming bitter. Kitty was the most overtly sensitive of them. During the worst of their parents' arguments, she would cry. Lydia pretended she was unaffected, but Elizabeth was the keeper of her secrets and knew that the strained atmosphere under which they lived left her anxious. It was a challenge to keep her from doing something impetuous, such as shouting at their parents. Elizabeth was afraid she would leap into the middle of one of their battles and end up as the object of her father's or mother's venom.

Elizabeth, who had been attempting to at least look like she was listening to Mrs Long, let her eyes wander, first to Jane, then to Mary. Her heart eased to see that they were well. Elizabeth could never leave her sisters to suffer at Longbourn without her consolation. Besides, she knew that if she were to marry and move away, it would be the work of a moment before her mother was thrusting all of her sisters into the arms of whatever man showed an interest in them, never stopping to discover if his intentions were honourable. It was up to Elizabeth to protect them, just as she had had to do for Jane.

It could be five years or more before her younger sisters were married—if they found husbands at all. By then, Elizabeth would be close to Charlotte's present age and unlikely to attract any worthy suitors. After all, if she had failed to do so at twenty, her chances of doing so as she grew older would be even dimmer.

Charlotte pulled her from her thoughts by saying, "Mr Darcy looks at you a great deal, Lizzy."

Elizabeth had not noticed when Mrs Long left them, but the older woman was half way across the room. Elizabeth laughed at Charlotte's suggestion, but when she looked over her shoulder, to where Charlotte's eyes indicated she would find the man, the rapid movement of his chin away from them suggested that he had indeed been watching them. Nevertheless, Elizabeth said, "I assure you that if he does—and I by no means believe it

—it is only to criticise. That man is pleased with nothing and no one."

"I *have* seen it, and he does not seem displeased with the view."

"Mr Darcy and I have not exchanged more than ten or twenty words in all the weeks he has been at Netherfield, and most of them have been 'good evening' or 'how do you do'. If you are implying that he has any kindly interest in me, you are mistaken. Please, let us talk about something else."

"Very well. I am going to open the instrument. You must start us off."

"Charlotte…"

"You know I shall insist, so, as the saying goes, keep your breath—"

"To cool my porridge. Very well."

DARCY WATCHED as Elizabeth Bennet walked to the pianoforte. He had been driven to observe her by curiosity and boredom—especially the latter, he assured himself. His research led him to believe that Miss Mary was new to society and uncomfortable, and Miss Elizabeth undertook to support and reassure her. Miss Elizabeth also often intervened to stop her mother from doing or saying something which would, no doubt, be inappropriate and embarrassing to the Miss Bennets. Darcy had no particular interest in Miss Elizabeth—how could he?—but she was…a compelling study. If he were being honest, he found it difficult not to want to know more about her.

A little bubble of excitement formed in his stomach when he realised Miss Elizabeth was going to perform, and he moved closer to the instrument. She sat and bent her head over the keys for a moment, exposing the back of her neck. The tips of Darcy's fingers tickled with the urge to dance over her skin and tug at the gold ribbon tangled in her curls. If he pulled it out, would her hair tumble down? How long was it? What would it feel like to run his hands through it? Would it smell like herbs or flowers?

In an effort to clear his thoughts, he took a large swallow of rather insipid punch. His efforts were for naught, because when Miss Elizabeth lifted her head and began to play and sing, he was enchanted and had to redouble his efforts to maintain his composure and not show that he was fascinated by her.

I will think rationally and not be swayed by...inconsequential matters. Such as the gentle curve of her— He bit the inside of his cheek in silent punishment. *From a technical standpoint, there is nothing remarkable about her performance, but the way she plays and her voice, so light and rich, is...captivating.* What really struck Darcy were her eyes. Not long after she started to sing, she looked in his direction. Their gazes locked for a moment, and he forgot how to breathe. Her eyes were dark and deep, and Darcy felt like he could fall into them and find *everything*—everything he had been searching for, even though he had been unaware of his need, everything he had dreamt of, just...*everything*.

So lost was he that the next thing he knew, she had finished the piece and was standing and gesturing to someone. Darcy pulled his lips into his mouth, licked them, and tried to calm his heart, which thudded loudly and painfully in his chest. Miss Mary joined her sister, and the two shared a brief whispered conversation. They then sat and played a French ballad together. Afterwards, Miss Elizabeth said what looked like encouraging words to Miss Mary, squeezed her hand, and nodded. Darcy's heart began to race again when she stood not two feet from him to watch her sister perform. As Miss Mary played a piece by Ignaz Pleyel, Darcy watched Miss Elizabeth. Her smile showed pride and she clapped once Miss Mary reached the end of the song.

A young couple he did not know approached the instrument and requested music to which they could dance. Sir William, walking by at just that moment, proclaimed it a capital idea, and Miss Mary agreed.

Miss Elizabeth remained where she was, and Darcy thought of his own sister.

Georgiana would benefit a great deal from having someone to encourage her the way Miss Elizabeth does her sister.

His urge to know more about her was overwhelming, and he stepped to her side and said, "Does the music not make you wish to dance?"

Her body, lean yet womanly, jerked as if he had startled her. She glanced at him with a polite smile and said, "Not at the moment. You, I know, can easily withstand such inducements, no matter the tune."

From any other lady, the words would have annoyed him, but Miss Elizabeth's teasing manner and the way her eyes sparkled made it impossible to be offended. He supposed his disinclination for dancing had been noticed at the assembly the previous month. Nevertheless, he had asked Miss Elizabeth to dance, and his offers were seldom refused. She gave him no excuse, did not even look at him again, and he did not believe that she, of all women, would ignore him as some sort of ploy to increase his interest and make him beg her to reconsider.

Which must mean she truly has no intention of dancing with me. He was not certain how to respond or even how to feel about her rejection. Her eyes remained on Miss Mary until the sound of Mrs Bennet's distinct voice drew his attention. Not all of the matron's words were clear, but Darcy heard her say 'Jane', 'Mr Bingley', and 'match' and could guess at the rest. Earlier, he had overheard her talking in an unkindly manner about Mr Bennet.

Miss Elizabeth's lips thinned, and she seemed to grow paler, and he struggled not to touch her arm or cheek to comfort her. With a hasty, "Excuse me," she left him, hurried to her mother, took the woman's elbow, and pulled her aside. Miss Elizabeth spoke for some time, shaking her head after Mrs Bennet responded. When her mother pointed at Miss Bennet and Bingley, Miss Elizabeth lowered her mother's hand, glanced at the couple, and spoke with some urgency. He assumed she was trying to convince her mother to hold her tongue.

For which we can all be grateful. He sighed. *I must have a word with Bingley about being more guarded lest he raise expectations he is unwilling to meet.* It would be an awkward conversation, and one he ought not to have—or have to have—with Bingley, who was, after all, his friend, not his younger brother or a dependent.

With the notion stored in his mind to attend to when

he and Bingley were alone, he returned to observing Miss Elizabeth Bennet. After several minutes, he forced his eyes away from her, and thought, *I shall have to take my own advice. While she appears to be an uncommon young lady and makes an interesting diversion, she could never be more than an acquaintance to me. I must treat her accordingly.*

FOUR

While Kitty practised the pianoforte the next day, Elizabeth reflected on the party at Lucas Lodge. Mary had played well, and Elizabeth had seen her blushing while speaking to young Charles Goulding, which was very sweet. Elizabeth was less pleased when she remembered how Mr Bingley had claimed Jane's company almost the entire evening, seemingly unmindful of how others would perceive his actions, including Jane.

I should not spend so much time thinking about Jane and Mr Bingley. But how can I not worry about Jane's reluctance to see other people for what they truly are? It is not only him. She believes Miss Bingley and Mrs Hurst consider her a friend, but if —when—they realise the neighbourhood will expect to see Jane installed as Netherfield's mistress, their affection will vanish in an instant. Why should they want her as a sister-in-law? They cannot approve of us. My mother and father are...unpleasant, and my sisters and I lack fortune or connexions. That matters to people like Mr Darcy and the Bingleys.

If anything would rob her of truly enjoying herself at a party, it was Mrs Bennet's presence. Elizabeth always kept one eye and ear on what her mother was doing and saying. When she was not gossiping about their neighbours, she would tell anyone who would listen about her unhappiness with Mr Bennet and how her daughters—save for Jane and Lydia—were a disappointment to her. Elizabeth had to be extra vigilant now that Jane was occupied with Mr Bingley and the gentleman's presence provided her mother with yet another 'interesting' subject on which to discourse.

Kitty hit a wrong note, and Elizabeth showed her how to correct her fingering.

In three days, Jane, Mary, and I shall dine at Purvis Lodge. Since my father and mother will spend the evening with Aunt Philips, I know I shall enjoy myself more than I did last night. She and her sisters would attend with the Lucases, and she could relax, knowing she need not worry about how either of her parents behaved. Her father could be just as mortifying as her mother; his sharp wit was seldom employed with tact or consideration.

Kitty reached the end of the piece, and Elizabeth gave her attention to her sister.

Kitty said, "Is it any better, Lizzy?"

"Yes, very much so." Elizabeth smiled at her. "What do you think about learning a duet with me? I have one we could prepare for next month."

Their aunt and uncle Gardiner would come to stay for at least a week to celebrate Christmas, and Kitty and

Lydia would be permitted to join some of the festivities. Singing carols was a favourite family activity.

"Do you think I am good enough?"

Elizabeth gave her a fond look. "We shall play so delightfully that everyone who hears us will faint with pleasure."

Kitty giggled, and Elizabeth retrieved the music.

DARCY REGARDED Miss Elizabeth as she laughed with her companion at the dinner table, the long, slender fingers of her right hand elegantly curled around the stem of her wine glass. They were dining at Purvis Lodge. Mrs Bennet was absent—for which he was heartily thankful—and Miss Elizabeth was noticeably more relaxed than he was used to seeing her. He did not know what she and the officer, Lieutenant Lowe, were talking about, but they had upheld a steady conversation the entire meal, leaving him to feel an irrational stab of jealousy.

She never shows such ease with me. Even when we greeted each other, she said no more than 'How do you do?'

Such thoughts were unworthy of him, but how could he not feel slighted, especially when she had refused to dance with him at Lucas Lodge.

But it is for the best, he reminded himself. *Her manner to me is appropriate; it shows that she understands she can never be anything but an acquaintance to me.*

During the separation of the sexes, Darcy had talked to Mr Lowe, hoping to learn what had occupied him and

Miss Elizabeth during dinner, but the lieutenant was too dimwitted to take Darcy's hints.

Darcy refrained from taking a place at the same table as Miss Elizabeth when they played cards. He did sit where he could continue his observations of her, however. Like at dinner, she talked and laughed easily with her companions. There was a certain lightness, almost a musical quality to her laugh that was lovely. Her whole person seemed to shine, to beckon him like a light in the darkness, drawing him ever closer. Surely he could not be the only one to notice that she was…different.

She is happy tonight; she practically shouts it to the world. It must be because of her mother's absence. She is still attentive to her sisters, especially Miss Mary, and I did see her watching Miss Bennet and Bingley for a while when we joined the ladies—but there is none of that anxiety I am used to sensing in her.

Not long after they started playing, Darcy wished he had allowed himself to be placed at her table. He wanted to know more about her, and he had given up an excellent opportunity to do it. Although they were separated by some fifteen feet, he could hear her voice and that laugh—oh, that laugh!—and he knew he would have enjoyed having her talk to him the way she was the two gentlemen sitting with her and to have her deep, enchanting eyes fixed on him, her soft lips turned upwards as she regarded him. She might blush when she realised, as she must, that he thought she was the loveliest—

And that was why it was better that they were separated.

As he took his leave of her later that night, their eyes met for just an instant.

"Miss Elizabeth," he said as he bowed. "I hope you have enjoyed yourself this evening."

"I have. Very much."

As she curtseyed, her eyes were already moving away from him and to her younger sister, who stood at her side. She offered Miss Mary a smile that was so soft and warm it was like a caress. Darcy murmured something or other to Miss Mary and left the ladies. He just managed not to expel a rush of air as he struggled to maintain his composure and prevent the heat from rising to his cheeks.

An interesting study or not, I must find a way to keep my distance from her.

❦

THE FOLLOWING MORNING, just before breakfast, Jane found Elizabeth alone in her bedchamber.

"Lizzy, I received a note from Miss Bingley. She has invited me to spend the day with her and Mrs Hurst. The gentlemen are dining with the officers. Do you think I should go?"

"If you wish to, why not?"

Jane's eyes flickered to the closed door of the room. "I was going to help Lydia with her French today, and you know I do not like to leave you alone when..." Her cheeks were suffused with colour, and she averted her eyes.

There had been rumblings of heightened discontent between Mr and Mrs Bennet for the last two days, and it was likely that their joint attendance at the Philipses the evening before had exacerbated the situation. It would be easier if Jane were there should their parents quarrel that morning, but Elizabeth was capable of shouldering the burden of caring for the younger girls on her own.

"Go and enjoy yourself," Elizabeth insisted. "I can help Lydia with French—I am better at it than you are anyway." She was teasing, hoping to ease Jane's conscience, and made a face that dared her to disagree.

"If you are sure?"

Elizabeth promised that she was, and the sisters went to join the rest of their family for the morning meal. Jane announced her plans for the day, and through the contrivance of Mrs Bennet, she was sent to Netherfield on horseback. A storm had been threatening even as they ate breakfast, and to no one's surprise, she was caught out in it. As a consequence of the continuing rain, Jane was forced to remain at Netherfield overnight. Mrs Bennet was delighted with the success of her scheme and spoke of nothing else through dinner and the evening.

ॐ

ELIZABETH RECEIVED news the next day that Jane had fallen ill with a cold and could not remove to Longbourn. Worried about her sister, Elizabeth decided to go to Netherfield Park and judge for herself how Jane fared. The three-mile journey gave Elizabeth time to cool her temper. She was frustrated that neither her mother nor her father appeared concerned about Jane. Mr Bennet had made a joke about her dying in pursuit of Mr Bingley, while Mrs Bennet had calculated how long Jane might remain in the gentleman's house.

Upon reaching the estate, Elizabeth was shown into the breakfast parlour, although she had asked to be brought directly to Jane. Her skirts were muddy, and her hair was in disarray; she did not feel she was fit to be seen.

"I am sorry to disturb you. I have come to enquire after Jane," she explained to the assembled party.

"You walked all this way?" Mrs Hurst said, which Miss Bingley followed with, "In the mud?"

Elizabeth pressed her lips together and nodded. She felt Mr Darcy's eyes on her, straightened her shoulders, and avoided looking in his direction.

"What a kind sister you are," Mr Bingley said. "I am sure Miss Bennet will be greatly relieved to see you. I shall have someone show you to her bedchamber." He led her to the door and so far into the hall that Elizabeth wondered if he might not end up walking her to Jane's room himself. "Anything that can be done for her comfort, we will do. *I* thought we ought to call the apothecary immediately, but my sisters said there was no need. I have not seen her, of course, so I have allowed myself to be guided by them."

Elizabeth was alarmed to find that Jane was a great deal sicker than she had supposed. Her throat was so sore that she could not speak without pain, and she had a fever. Elizabeth did what she could for her sister and requested that a note be sent to the apothecary.

When Mr Jones saw her, he pronounced that Jane had a violent cold and should not be moved for at least several days. As much as Elizabeth hated the idea of Jane remaining under the same roof as Mr Bingley, knowing it could only encourage her sister to further open her heart to him, her greater fear was injuring Jane's health by convincing her to return to Longbourn.

Elizabeth and the apothecary went to the parlour, where the Bingleys, Mrs Hurst, and Mr Darcy were gathered, and told them the news. The ladies were shocked, Mr Darcy looked grave, and Mr Bingley became pale and, to Elizabeth's eye, looked a little confused, as though he could not believe he was receiving such dreadful news. For a moment, she wondered if he might have feelings for her sister that went beyond a desire to amuse himself while he was in the neighbourhood. She longed to believe that he could love Jane—indeed, who could not?—but doubted he would go against his family's disapproval, perhaps even his own inclinations and common sense, and marry her.

Elizabeth thanked Mr Jones, who then departed. Dismissing the question of Mr Bingley's feelings, her concern returned to Jane. She loathed the very notion of leaving her under the care of Mrs Hurst and Miss Bingley. She was nibbling on her lower lip and tapping her fingers on her leg when Mr Bingley said, "Miss Elizabeth, you must remain. I am certain you will want to tend to Miss Bennet yourself, and she would take comfort in your presence."

His simple words, offered with so much warmth, spoke well of him. When she turned to offer him a grateful smile, she noticed that Mr Darcy stood beside him, evidently interested in the conversation.

With reluctance, she said, "I would like to, but I cannot. I am needed at home."

"Whatever for?" Miss Bingley asked from the sofa, where she and Mrs Hurst sat. "You have sisters enough to undertake whatever chores you must do to maintain the house."

"My younger sisters need me," Elizabeth said without fully meaning to. Addressing Mr Bingley, she said, "Perhaps my sister Mary might come in my stead. I apologise for the unusual request. I appreciate your invitation, and I do not wish to tax your sisters' time or that of your servants in tending to Jane. While I know you would take excellent care of her, she is not your responsibility."

Proving his amiability, Mr Bingley said, "Since you are unable to stay yourself, we would be glad to have Miss Mary."

Mr Bingley offered his carriage to bring Elizabeth to Longbourn and escort Mary to Netherfield. Elizabeth accepted and went to explain the arrangements to Jane.

§

DARCY WATCHED Miss Elizabeth leave the parlour. He attributed the heaviness in his body and the grimace he knew he wore to anxiety, not disappointment that she was returning to Longbourn. Mr Jones's report on Miss Bennet had been alarming, and he prayed she made a quick recovery.

Why she rode here when it threatened rain is beyond my comprehension. It is no wonder she fell ill. But what could Miss Elizabeth mean by saying her younger sisters need her? He had yet to see the two sisters who were not out. If one or both of them suffered some malady that required additional care, surely he would have heard. In the absence of such an excuse, why could not Miss Elizabeth remain, leaving the two youngest to Mrs Bennet, Miss Mary, and their servants?

From behind him, Darcy heard the ladies chattering. He did not attend to what they said, but the addition of Bingley's voice, deep and agitated, told him enough. They were gossiping about the Bennets again. Miss Bingley and Mrs Hurst had had a great deal to say about Miss Elizabeth's appearance after she left them in the breakfast room—none of it kind—and he expected they had resumed their criticisms.

I begin to suspect— No, I am certain; Miss Elizabeth is a far worthier lady than either of them. If only she had agreed to stay at Netherfield. Then I might have been able to make out her character and put my nagging curiosity about her to rest once and for all.

He suppressed a sigh that he knew would have drawn comment and joined the others.

FIVE

Darcy hardly noticed Mary Bennet for the first two days she was at Netherfield. To be fair, she spent most of her time with Miss Bennet who, while remaining ill, was in no danger, for which he was thankful. When Miss Mary was with them, Mrs Hurst and Miss Bingley ignored her, which did not surprise him. Miss Mary appeared to be a shy creature, not entirely unlike his sister, and was likely glad for the lack of notice. Mrs Hurst and Miss Bingley might easily overwhelm her, as they did Georgiana, whom they praised excessively.

On the other hand, he suspected Miss Elizabeth would give them their own back, and then some. *If she had remained instead of her younger sister, we might have...had diverting conversations, and I could have—*

Nothing. He could have nothing. There was no point to getting to know her further. *If anything, showing an interest in her, even if only to satisfy my curiosity, would be a mistake.* Had he not warned Bingley about guarding his behaviour with Miss Bennet?

Not that he listened, Darcy reflected as he paced back and forth on the terrace one afternoon during an interlude in the rain. *He likes her and is convinced his feelings for her are different from those he has had for the many other 'angels' he has met these last years. Her lack of connexions means nothing to him. His sisters, however, will not stand for it. If, that is, he decides he wants to marry her.*

Bingley would have to show more strength of character than he usually did; Miss Bingley and Mrs Hurst would, no doubt, try to dissuade him taking such a step. As for Darcy, he knew Bingley could make a much more advantageous match—perhaps even Georgiana in three or four years—but it was Bingley's choice. He could not say he liked Mr and Mrs Bennet. Whenever he saw the gentleman, he seemed bored with life and disdainful of his company, especially that of his wife. Mrs Bennet was a gossip and would be much worse if a certain lovely young lady did not spend so much of her time making sure her mother held her tongue. However, Darcy knew no evil of the Bennet girls; they were pleasant and polite.

It was on the third day of the Bennet ladies' stay that Darcy and Miss Mary had their first conversation. He was reading in the library when she entered and began to examine Bingley's meagre collection of books. She did not notice his presence, and after observing her for a minute or two, he said her name, being sure to speak gently so as not to startle her. Nevertheless, she jumped.

"Oh. Mr Darcy." She clutched a book to her chest and

regarded him with rounded eyes. "I did not mean to disturb you, sir."

"You have not, I assure you. I hope Miss Bennet continues to improve?"

"She does, thank you. She is sleeping at the moment."

Seeking to relieve her evident awkwardness, Darcy said, "And you sought a quiet place to read? As you see, so have I. Please." He gestured to a chair near the fireplace. The weather continued to be rainy, and the house felt chilly and damp unless one was close to the fire's warmth. "I have asked the housekeeper for tea. I shall request a cup for you." With that, he went to the door and spoke to a servant before taking a seat across from Miss Mary.

"You need not take such trouble for me," she said. "I can—"

"Not at all," he interjected. "The ladies and Mr Hurst intended to play cards, and Bingley is with his steward. If you wish a quiet place to read, you have chosen wisely." Darcy was aware that he was too forward, but he had a strong desire to speak to Miss Mary about Miss Elizabeth.

Tea and a plate of biscuits were brought in. When Miss Mary tried to say that, really, she did not mean to intrude on his solitude, he insisted the snack would do her good.

Darcy spoke to her about the volume she had chosen and what she liked to read for a few minutes and confirmed his belief that she was shy and lacked confidence.

"Lizzy tells me I ought not to always read such

serious things," she said, having described her most recent two books, one on etiquette and the other a collection of sermons. Her cheeks became rosy, and she looked at the cup she held in her lap. "I do not mean to sound as though I am criticising her; she is quite right. I-I *do* tend to be too sombre and imagine I would be very dull if she did not encourage me to explore other types of books and…"

"And?" he asked when her voice trailed off.

"Laugh, I suppose. Lizzy likes to laugh and find the humour in everything." A shadow crossed her face, and at a whisper, she said, "As much as she can, in any case."

"Miss Elizabeth has struck me as a happy sort of person." *Yet also a very careful one.*

"Lizzy always says she is not formed for ill-humour. She believes contentment is a decision, not a circumstance."

Darcy thought about the evening at Purvis Lodge. It was the easiest he had seen her, the most relaxed and happy, and he wondered what burdens she might bear that so often robbed her of her desire to laugh. It struck him that for whatever happened at Longbourn, Miss Elizabeth, while serious, was never peevish or ill-humoured. *As I am wont to be.* He moved from that thought immediately.

"You have two other sisters, I believe?"

Miss Mary nodded. "Catherine and Lydia. They are not yet out."

He asked their ages and explained that he had a sister who, like Miss Catherine, was sixteen. "She would be envious of you. She has always wanted a sister. I have wished that for her, too, especially an older sister who might...guide her. She is shy, and with no mother, feels the want of feminine company."

Miss Mary smiled. "We are very fortunate, us younger ones, to have such excellent older sisters. Lizzy especially."

"Oh?" Darcy resisted the urge to lean closer.

The colour on her cheeks deepened, and he had the impression she had not intended to say so much. He did his best to arrange his features so that he appeared interested without being eager. Perhaps because she did not know how to extricate herself from the conversation, she continued speaking.

"Lizzy takes prodigious care of us and has since she was younger than I am. Jane is wonderful, but Lizzy is... sensible and energetic and quick-witted. She makes sure that we learn what we need to know and that— Well, she is very dependable. You could not find a kinder, more loyal sister in the whole kingdom."

This was a glowing recommendation, and it was evident that Miss Mary loved and looked up to Miss Elizabeth. It did not tell Darcy *why* Miss Elizabeth expended so much effort caring for her sisters or watching her parents when they were in company, but he had discomfited his companion enough and changed the subject. In a few minutes, their tea finished, they both turned their attention to their books. Try as he might to avoid it, Darcy's thoughts often drifted to a place three miles away where a certain beguiling young lady resided.

JANE AND MARY remained at Netherfield for five days. The expected storm between Mr and Mrs Bennet happened during their absence, fortunately when it was not raining. As soon as Elizabeth heard the first angry words, she, Kitty, and Lydia went for a walk. They returned after an hour, dirty but refreshed and glad they missed their parents' latest battle. Elizabeth wondered if she should keep a record of the number of such occurrences; it seemed to her that they were increasing in frequency, especially the severest ones, but it could be that it only appeared that way because she was tired of hearing them, tired of her parents.

Mrs Bennet was disappointed that Jane had not found a way to remain a full week under Mr Bingley's roof, but Elizabeth was glad to have all of her sisters with her again.

"Was it very difficult?" Jane asked when they were alone.

"Not at all. I am tempted to say that we did not miss you, but that is too teasing even for me. Instead, I will say that we managed to stay busy and avoid growing to hate the sight of each other, even though we were mostly restricted to indoor activities. I am happy to see blue sky today. What a lot of rain we have had! But tell me, how are you? You still look pale."

"I am recovered, although I am tired in that way one becomes when they have been confined to bed for several days. If the weather holds, I hope we can take a long walk tomorrow. That will do me the world of good."

"It would do us all good. Now, shall I ask about the company? Did you spend much time with Mr Bingley?"

Jane blushed and lowered her eyes. "The ladies were very kind, though I only saw Mr Bingley in the evenings, and it was only the last two days when I was strong enough to go down. You know my opinion of him. You are wrong about him, Lizzy; I am certain of it."

Elizabeth was dubious but said, "I would be very pleased to discover it. Truly, Jane."

Jane clasped her hand and smiled.

Later the same day, Elizabeth asked Mary how she had fared at Netherfield. Mary thought it had gone well, but she admitted to wanting more occupation.

"I cannot understand how other ladies fill the long hours of the day, especially when confronted with such poor weather."

"Did you see a great deal of Miss Bingley and Mrs Hurst?"

Mary shook her head. "They sat with Jane, but never for more than a few minutes at a time. At dinner and in the evening, they and Mr Hurst said hardly anything to me. I believe they were content to pretend I was not there at all."

"I am afraid we are not fashionable or high enough to suit their tastes. Jane at least has her beauty to recommend her. Next you will say that Mr Bingley was affable." Mary nodded. "And what of Mr Darcy? I hope he treated you as he ought."

Elizabeth was prepared to hear that he had been rude, thus she was surprised by her sister's response.

"He did. Mr Darcy is not as lively as Mr Bingley, but he was friendly to me. I think his reticence makes it easy to mistake his manner."

"I am pleased to know he was kind to you."

"He was. We were in the library together one afternoon. I had gone in to find a book to read and chose a volume of poetry. He made a point of asking me about it the next day, and even helped me understand it. I know he has not been the most agreeable neighbour, but perhaps some of that may be due to his feeling awkward amongst so many new people."

Elizabeth laughed. "Mary, he was very rude at the assembly."

Mary hastened to agree, adding, "I do not excuse him, and I wish for his sake he made more of an effort, but I feel like I discovered a different side of him."

Elizabeth was not inclined to discuss the gentleman further and changed the subject.

That night, listening to Lydia's even breathing as they lay together in bed, her thoughts returned to Mary's words about Mr Darcy.

I am relieved he showed Mary the consideration she deserves; I wish he would do the same with everyone he met. What a puzzling man.

⁂

THE BENNET SISTERS walked into Meryton two days later. There was a touch of ice in the wind that hinted at the coming winter, and the world had become greyer overnight, with bare trees and the absence of autumn flowers to add colour to the paths they walked along. Entering the town, the aroma of fresh bread and pies from the bakery mixed with those of smoke and horse. They were greeted by two officers Jane, Elizabeth, and Mary had met—Mr Denny and Captain Carter—and introduced to Mr Wickham, an old friend of Mr Denny's who had lately joined the militia. After accepting her part of the introduction, Mary stepped to the side to stand with Kitty and Lydia.

Elizabeth found the addition of so many new gentlemen to their society made the usual evening parties livelier and more interesting, though they had not been in town long and the novelty might wear off before the regiment removed elsewhere. Mrs Bennet was disappointed that none of the officers appeared to be in a position to take a wife, with the exception of Colonel Forster, who was rumoured to be betrothed. Since Elizabeth had no intention of marrying, she only considered whether they were good company. She suspected that Mr Wickham would soon find himself to be a popular guest. He was very handsome and had a refined air that made Elizabeth curious to know more about him.

"From where do you hail, Mr Wickham?" she asked.

Before he could respond, their attention was drawn by two approaching riders. Seeing Jane's eyes light up and her lips form a smile, Elizabeth supposed one of them must be Mr Bingley. Sure enough, the gentleman's voice called out a greeting, and she turned to look at him.

"Miss Bennet, Darcy and I were on our way to Long-bourn to enquire after your health. I can see that you are well."

Mr Darcy was beside his friend, and Elizabeth was shocked to see his expression harden. He had looked on the verge of greeting her, then closed his mouth so forcefully she imagined she could hear it slam shut. He was looking at Mr Wickham, whose countenance had gone ashen.

Without so much as a word, Mr Darcy turned his horse and rode away.

Elizabeth did not know what to make of the encounter. That Mr Darcy was furious seemed obvious, and Mr Wickham... That was more difficult to determine since she had just made his acquaintance. Seeing that Elizabeth had observed the encounter, he gave a nervous laugh, and, although he faced her, his eyes darted up and down the street.

"As you can see, Darcy and I are not friends."

Elizabeth smiled politely, but would not ask him to explain the connexion, no matter that she burned with curiosity. Instead, she said, "If you will excuse me," and went to join her younger sisters. She asked Mary to stay with Jane, while she, Kitty, and Lydia went to the circulating library, deciding to meet at the confectionery afterwards.

"I shall treat us all," she announced cheerfully. "I believe we deserve it."

As they walked off, Kitty asked, "Who was the new gentleman, Lizzy?"

Lydia said, "He was the handsomest gentleman I have ever seen. Did I hear Mr Denny say he is to join the militia? I hope we see him in a red coat." She and Kitty regarded each other and giggled.

With more patience than she felt, Elizabeth said, "I agree that he is handsome, but—"

"There are more important qualities a man must possess," Lydia interjected as if repeating a lesson learnt by rote.

Apparently, Elizabeth had expressed the sentiment too many times, but she could not regret it, not as long as she recalled what might have happened to Jane. "It can be too easy to overlook a man's failings when he wears such an attractive face and has pleasing manners."

Kitty asked, "Will you see him at Aunt Philips's tonight?"

"If you do," Lydia said, "you must find out everything you can about him and promise to tell us."

Without letting her sisters see her, Elizabeth lifted her eyes to the heavens.

"I shall never complain about anything ever again once I am old enough to be out."

Kitty's tone was so much like a whine that Elizabeth had to bite her tongue not to reprimand her. Although both girls agreed that they were too young to enter society, the excitement of having a regiment in Meryton had made them discontented.

Elizabeth said, "You might not like it as much as you suppose you will. You do not need officers or evenings playing cards with our neighbours to amuse yourselves. I would not mind fewer of both."

In the minute it took to reach the library, she proposed several schemes to occupy them and encouraged them to think of others—both those they could do on their own while she, Jane, and Mary were out and those the five of them could do together.

SIX

Elizabeth was sitting alone on a settee that evening when, to her surprise, Mr Wickham took the empty place beside her. The party had begun above an hour earlier, and without purposely looking for him, Elizabeth had noticed the new lieutenant chatting with the other guests as if he had known them for weeks.

"Are you enjoying yourself, Mr Wickham?" she enquired.

"Very much. Denny told me I would find the society friendly, and I have. I was much in need of cheering. I believe that alone convinced me to return with him when we met in town last week."

He seemed to be inviting her to ask about the meaning behind his cryptic remark, which was odd given that, altogether, they had spoken no more than two minutes. "I am glad. A small society such as ours benefits from having new people amongst us." She could not stop herself from adding, "Mr Bingley has lately leased a nearby estate, as you may have heard. Perhaps you have met him before. He was the gentleman with Mr Darcy this morning."

"Ah, yes, Darcy." Mr Wickham cleared his throat and took a sip of punch. "Has he been here long?"

"Almost a month."

"Are you friends?"

"No, not particularly."

Mr Wickham's features softened, and Elizabeth had the impression that he approved of her response. When he asked if Mr Darcy had made many friends in the neighbourhood, she was uneasy, in part because of Mary's recent experiences with him.

Before she could find an appropriate response, John Lucas, who stood nearby, said, "No one here likes Mr Darcy. What a disagreeable fellow! Feels he is better than all of us."

One of John's friends called his name, and he left them without another word. Elizabeth was on the point of standing and excusing herself when Mr Wickham spoke.

"I wish I could say it surprises me. You wonder at my interest, Miss Elizabeth, and the cold manner of our greeting earlier today. I have known Darcy my entire life. My father was the late Mr Darcy's steward, and he and I grew up together. It has been years since I could think well of him. His pride is extreme and makes him tedious company."

Mr Wickham talked about them playing together as boys and going to school and university together. Elizabeth knew she should stop him. She was at turns disgusted that he was confiding so much in a stranger, fascinated by his story, and ashamed that she continued to listen. A part of her hoped he would say something to help her understand Mr Bingley's character, but he did not.

"The late Mr Darcy was my godfather and excessively fond of me. As we left boyhood behind and Darcy saw his father's affection for me, his jealousy grew, as did his contempt for those he sees as beneath him in consequence. Is Miss Darcy with him?"

"Miss Darcy? His sister?" When Mr Wickham nodded, she said "I did not even know he had a sister."

He sighed and his lips turned downward, but she glimpsed a lack of sincerity in his eyes. "Ah, that is a shame. Not that he would have let us meet. I was always a favourite of hers. Darcy has had the charge of her since their father's death five years ago. Georgiana is young— just fifteen—and I fear she is growing to be just like him. Perhaps it is better that I shall have no opportunity to see her. Had things transpired the way they were supposed to, had Darcy done as his father asked, I would have been a neighbour to them. He did me a grave wrong, Miss Elizabeth." He shook his head slowly and sighed again.

Elizabeth had heard enough, too much for her comfort. She had no interest in being his confidant and stood. "You will excuse me, Mr Wickham, I feel I ought to—"

Mr Wickham sprang to his feet and stayed her with a hand on her arm. Her eyes darted to where he held her and back to his face as she extricated her limb.

"I apologise, Miss Elizabeth." He offered her a weak smile. "Seeing him so unexpectedly has brought up old hurts. I thought I had conquered them, but…" For at least the third time, he sighed.

Elizabeth said, "I am sorry for you, Mr Wickham. I hope you will not have to meet him often while the two of you remain in the neighbourhood." She gave a curt nod and went to join Jane and Charlotte Lucas.

WHEN BINGLEY ANNOUNCED that he had decided to host a ball at Netherfield, Miss Bingley and Mrs Hurst did their best to argue him out of it. However, Bingley held firm, claiming it was absolutely necessary.

"We have received such a warm welcome. This is the least we can do to repay our neighbours," Bingley said. "It will be fun."

They were in the withdrawing room when the conversation took place. Darcy caught Miss Bingley peering at him before she turned back to her brother. "Some amongst us will take no pleasure in the event, Charles." Her tone hinted at a warning.

Bingley said, "If you mean Darcy—"

"Then you are mistaken," he interjected, eliciting a startled squeak from Miss Bingley. "Bingley is correct that this is an excellent way to thank your new neighbours and earn their goodwill. As the residents of one of the principal houses in the neighbourhood, Miss Bingley, many will wish, even expect, you to host balls and other large parties which are not easily accommodated in smaller homes. I trust your steward and housekeeper have spoken to you about arranging festive events for Netherfield's tenants and dependents, Bingley?" Darcy understood his duty as a landowner, and, as much as he had no particular wish to attend a ball at Netherfield, he knew Bingley ought to give one.

Bingley opened his mouth to reply, but before he could, Miss Bingley, her face red, said, "But you never!"

Darcy understood what she meant, even though she had expressed herself poorly. "Without a suitable hostess, I have not had a ball for my neighbours, but I regularly hold amusements for my tenants and those in the local community."

That ended the argument, as he had hoped it would.

Bingley asked Darcy to go with them when they delivered invitations to particular neighbours, including those at Longbourn, but he declined in favour of writing letters. He owed Georgiana a reply, and he told her about the Bennet sisters. He gripped the pen tightly, staring at the page, resisting the urge to write something extra about Miss Elizabeth. Next, he jotted a few lines to his cousin Colonel Fitzwilliam to tell him about seeing Wickham.

Damn it. Why did Wickham have to be here? What am I to do? Just as had been the case for the last five months, he felt torn between his desire to protect his sister and to expose Wickham's perfidy. Georgiana always weighed most heavily in his thoughts, and he knew that—again— he would hold his tongue. *Perhaps there is something Fitzwilliam can do, some influence in the military he can use to see the piece of vermin sent wherever he is most likely to get lost, if not lose his life. He deserves nothing better.*

Darcy threw his pen on the table, a splash of ink

marring the bottom of the paper. He walked around the room several times to clear his mind, then returned to the desk to attend to his letters.

&

THE FOLLOWING day brought with it brilliant blue skies and the warmest weather they had seen in a fortnight. Enough time had passed since it last rained for the ground to dry completely, and Darcy and Bingley decided to take advantage of it by going for a long ride. The air was crisp and held the faint odour of rotting leaves. They spoke now and again, but for the most part, the only sound was that of hooves striking the ground, the wind rustling through the trees, and animals scurrying to avoid them.

Then they heard feminine voices and a sprinkling of laughter. Bingley glanced at him, grinned, and turned his horse towards the sound. Darcy followed, wondering if Bingley had recognised one of the speakers or if he was making assumptions based on geography. It did not matter when, a moment later, he saw the Bennet sisters. Bingley was already slipping off his horse and calling out a greeting. Darcy's eyes immediately found Miss Elizabeth. He had the impression that she scowled as she regarded her older sister and Bingley, but she was soon smiling politely, and he thought no more about it. Her cheeks were rosy, no doubt due to the autumn weather, and he felt an urge to cup them with his bare hands to share his warmth with her.

Darcy dismounted, and Miss Elizabeth introduced him to her two youngest sisters. When the walk continued, Bingley fell into place beside Miss Bennet; Miss Mary stayed just behind them, and within a minute, the trio had put some distance between them and the rest of the party. Miss Elizabeth appeared to want to join them but was held back by her younger sisters. Miss Catherine and Miss Lydia were soon skipping ahead of him and Miss Elizabeth, their long hair swinging back and forth. When the two girls laughed, Miss Elizabeth's features softened into a gentle smile.

"I believe you have a sister who is much younger than you are?" she said.

The sound of her voice, and the subject of her question, startled him. He had been half lost in contemplating how fond she was of her sisters and how much he wished Georgiana had someone like her in her life.

"I do. Georgiana is lately turned sixteen."

She looked at her sisters again. "It can be a trying age, between childhood and adulthood."

Darcy's thoughts flew to the near-disaster with Wickham, and he thanked God yet again that he had decided to go to Ramsgate when he did. If he had not... But he had arrived in time to prevent their elopement, and it did no good to think about it.

At length, he said, "It is. My father died five years ago, my mother many years before that. I am my sister's guardian, along with a cousin. It is a great responsibility." With trepidation, he added, "I expect you understand what I mean."

She gave him a puzzled look. "I can *imagine* how it would be, but understand? No. Why would I?"

He cleared his throat. "I-I only meant that— It seems

you take a great deal of care of your sisters. You worry about them more than I would expect to see."

Her manner was diffident when she replied, "My mother is not inclined to oversee their education. I did not like to see it neglected."

Darcy regarded her as she spoke, and something about her guarded manner suggested that there was a great deal she was not saying. But it was not his business, and he had much better enjoy his conversation with Miss Elizabeth, which was one of the first they had shared without being constantly interrupted. It was just that he truly believed she did more for her sisters than she was admitting, and he admired her for stepping into such a role when she was so young.

Admit it, man. You admire a great deal more about her than that.

Searching for something to say that was less likely to cause her to flee his company, he said, "If I may ask, who told you about my sister?"

"Mr Wickham did." She glanced at him. "He was quite free with his opinion of you, to be honest."

Anger flared through him, rendering him silent. *Wickham! Sharing his lies about me already—and to Miss Elizabeth of all people!*

When she continued speaking, her tone was light, but her words shocked him so much that he nearly stumbled. "He asked if we were friends. I said no, and that was all the invitation he needed to tell me that you had thrown him over, despite having been childhood companions."

"Of what crimes did he charge me?" Darcy tried to keep his tone even, but he knew he had failed. Miss Elizabeth turned her expressive, dark eyes on him for a moment before returning them to her sisters.

"None. Our conversation was not long, but what he said was more than I felt comfortable hearing. He called you proud and said he imagined that you had done little to make yourself agreeable to the neighbourhood. Oh, he did say that you would not allow him to see your sister, although she had always been fond of him. I did not ask him for any of this information, Mr Darcy, and I cannot like that he confided so much to a stranger. Since you have a history with him, it may not surprise you. Indeed, I suspect from your manner that it has not."

Darcy took a moment to reflect and calm himself before he spoke. "No, it does not. I regret that he so importuned you." *At least he refrained from telling her that I neglected my father's wishes to give him a valuable living.*

It stung that she would say so casually that they were not friends. He cleared his throat. "Do you believe he painted an accurate portrayal of me? Have I been so very disagreeable?"

Her laugh was deep and from her belly. She did not answer but only shook her head and said his name.

Seeing that she had no intention of answering his question, he said, "Please tell me. Do not fear offending me." His tone was stiff, but he could not help it. His head swam with the notion that, while he was realising that he liked her far more than he ought, she would not even call him a friend.

She stopped walking for a moment and regarded him. Seeing that she remained reluctant to speak, he repeated his entreaty.

Her brow furrowed, and she looked at her sisters

before she sighed, resumed walking, and said, "The first night any of us met you, you sat next to Mrs Long for a half an hour and did not talk to her. You danced with only Mrs Hurst and Miss Bingley, even though there were not enough men and a number of ladies lacked partners. Every time I have seen you in company, you have stood by a wall, on your own, saying as little as possible. How could it not give the people here the impression that you have no interest in befriending anyone?"

Darcy felt his cheeks heat and prayed she would not notice; it would only heighten his embarrassment. "I-it is not that at all. I am seldom comfortable amongst people I do not know well. I cannot catch the flow of the conversation or-or…"

She bit her lips together as though to stop herself from laughing. "You are an intelligent, educated man, Mr Darcy, and I suspect you have often been in company far grander and more numerous than what Meryton has to offer you. I should think it would be no trouble to ask a lady to dance and make a few inconsequential comments on the room, or to enquire of an older lady if she has children or the like."

When Miss Catherine and Miss Lydia gestured to her, she said, "If you will excuse me. I must attend my sisters."

She offered him a quick nod and left him to stare after her. Darcy stood still for a moment, one hand clutching his horse's reins, and watched as Miss Elizabeth smiled at her sisters as they spoke with animation and showed her something. They walked on.

Darcy trailed behind, considering Miss Elizabeth, her

words, and his behaviour. He had to admit that she was right; he had done little to make himself pleasant to the people of Meryton, especially the ladies.

I suppose it is because I heard so many of them gossiping about me the night of the assembly. It is no different in town, but is more tolerable there because I am just one of many whose lives are dissected in all their minutiae. Here, I am a stranger, and there are fewer of us who are unknown—just Bingley, his family, and me.

It would be easy to say that anxiety about Georgiana's recovery from the affair in Ramsgate had soured his mood before he ever came to Netherfield, but it was a weak excuse. He had not bothered to be pleasant because, as she had rightly implied, he *had* thought the company beneath his notice.

If I am not careful, I shall become like Lady Catherine. I would despise myself if I allow that to happen. Again, anger coursed through him, though this time it was joined by sorrow and regret that his own actions meant a lady of Miss Elizabeth's quality might agree with Wickham or find his tales of woe credible. *It will not do. The most effective counter to Wickham's lies is to show myself to be a true gentleman.*

As they continued their walk, he regarded Miss Elizabeth and contemplated how her opinion had become so important to him. When he had first arrived at Netherfield, he cared not what anyone in the neighbourhood thought of him and never would have dreamt that the day would come when he was near-desperate to show that he was worthy of them. *Not of them, of her. But why and to what end?*

It was twenty or thirty minutes before he had

another opportunity to speak to her. The party had reassembled at the top of a hill from which there was a delightful view of the surrounding countryside. Miss Elizabeth stood to one side, her hands clasped behind her back, looking over the fields and cottages in the distance. Darcy joined her, and she offered him a polite smile though it lacked the genuine welcome he longed to see. He realised that her manner to him these last weeks had been similar, but he had not seen it, had not wanted to admit that her regard was becoming important to him.

Smoke plumed from chimneys, and to one side, he saw Netherfield Park. The landscape was speckled with the deep green of evergreen trees. After a moment of silence, he said, "You are correct, Miss Elizabeth. I ought to have done better, exerted myself more, despite my discomfort. I can only promise to attempt to rectify my behaviour in the future."

Miss Elizabeth regarded him for a moment before nodding.

"About Wickham," he said, "I wrote to my cousin, who is a colonel in the regulars, to tell him that he was here. I hope he will use his influence to ensure Wickham is not in a position where he can injure anyone. I am troubled that he spreads lies about me. Please believe that much of what he says is false. His behaviour is not that of a gentleman. I can only offer Bingley to speak for my credibility, but I hope you will be careful around him, as will your sisters."

Her brow furrowed. "I see. I thank you for the warning, sir."

They again lapsed into silence, which he broke by asking if the Bennets would attend the Netherfield ball.

"We certainly shall."

His mouth was dry, and he ran his tongue over his teeth. "Would you do me the honour of dancing with me?"

Her eyes, sparkling with mirth, met his. She seemed to be fighting not to smile, and he thought—prayed—that she regarded him with something like approval. "Are you practising your civility, Mr Darcy?"

He bowed his head, though he knew it was more than that. While he would ask other ladies to dance at the ball because he knew he ought to, he *wanted* to dance with Miss Elizabeth.

She said, "I accept—for any set other than the first."

Before he could ask why, Miss Bennet's voice called out, "Lizzy, we should return to Longbourn."

Miss Elizabeth again smiled at him—and he fancied that this time, it was not mere politeness—then went to join her sisters.

Darcy's answering smile lingered. As the party retraced their steps, he reflected, *I believe the last time I felt like smiling like this was when I watched her play and sing at Lucas Lodge. Then when we were at Purvis Lodge. And when I saw her in Meryton before I noticed Wickham.*

He watched her walking beside Miss Mary, the gentle wave of her skirts almost hypnotic. He knew he was in danger, yet…

Yet if this is danger, it feels remarkably agreeable.

SEVEN

The evening before the Netherfield Ball, after Mr Bennet had retreated to his library, Jane invited Elizabeth to her room by using a feeble-sounding excuse about selecting jewellery. Mary was writing a letter, and the younger girls were occupied with Mrs Bennet. Elizabeth sat on the bed and watched as Jane stood at the dressing table, poking through her things. At length, Jane spoke, keeping her back to Elizabeth.

"Lizzy, have you ever thought about marriage? We have never really talked about it, and-and I would like…" She turned to face Elizabeth. "I want to get married, leave Longbourn, and have a home of my own and children."

A sinking feeling in her chest kept Elizabeth silent. She had long accepted that Jane would marry—she truly wished it for her—but this was about Mr Bingley.

"I know you have felt we needed to protect the girls from—" Jane's voice cracked, and she took a moment to swallow before continuing. "They are not children any longer; they do not need us the way they did four or five years ago. Mama so wants to bring Kitty and Lydia out, and I know the girls would like it."

Elizabeth leapt to her feet. "You cannot seriously believe—?"

"We were their age when we went into society, and it was not so very bad."

Elizabeth wanted to scream but kept her voice steady. "It was *terrible*, Jane, and the girls are too young. They are no longer children, I agree, but not yet women and mature enough for what awaits them, even with a more diligent chaperone than Mama." A sudden thought occurred to Elizabeth. "Has Mr Bingley made you an offer?"

Jane's cheeks turned bright pink. "Not...not yet."

"But you are convinced that he will? I tell you, Jane, I am not. His sisters would despise it, and Mr Darcy—"

"Mr Darcy?" Jane's voice was almost as shrill as their mother's when she demanded, "What about him? You talked to him a great deal today. Do not think I did not notice just because Mr Bingley and I walked together."

Elizabeth held up her hands, palms out, and took several calming breaths. "Jane, please recall that you have only known Mr Bingley for two months, and while he gives every appearance of amiability, he is the only one at Netherfield who does. I remember another gentleman who was just as handsome and engaging, and after what happened with him, I urge you to exercise more caution."

Jane's chin quivered, and tears filled her eyes.

Elizabeth closed the distance between them, embraced her sister, and whispered, "I truly hope Mr Bingley is worthy of your regard, but until there is greater proof that he is, I beg you would guard yourself, Jane. I do not want to see you suffer disappointment or derision—or worse—should he not prove to be all that you think he is."

After a moment, Jane nodded and stepped away. She turned her back to Elizabeth and said, "Why do you not join Mama and the girls? I will be down in a few minutes."

Elizabeth allowed Jane her moment of privacy and prayed it helped reconcile Jane to thinking about Mr Bingley as nothing more than a pleasant acquaintance. *One who I suspect will not long remain in the neighbourhood.*

BY THE NEXT MORNING, Elizabeth had succeeded in putting the conversation with Jane out of her mind. A private ball was an uncommon event and too delicious not to savour. For one night, she could set aside her worries.

If nothing else, I anticipate seeing if Mr Darcy remains determined to be more sociable!

She had been surprised by his invitation to dance. *Perhaps he only wishes to show that I was mistaken about him. Yet...* Something told her it was an ungenerous thought. *I shall have to judge for myself whether there is more to it than that.*

There was something about Mr Darcy that made her

sense of curiosity tingle. She supposed it had something to do with his seemingly quick decision to improve his manners once she had explained how he was perceived by others. It spoke well of him. Not many men, especially those like Mr Darcy, who was rich and doubtless had excellent connexions, would do the same.

She said nothing to her sisters about him asking her to dance. She did not truly believe he would forget or decide not to honour their agreement. Nevertheless, she preferred to keep it to herself.

Longbourn was buzzing with activity as Jane, Elizabeth, and Mary prepared for the evening. Kitty and Lydia skipped between the sisters' bedchambers, offering their assistance.

With some envy in her voice, Lydia said to Elizabeth, "You will get to dance with all the gentlemen. The officers will be there, and Mr Bingley must have ever so many friends coming from town. Perhaps you will fall madly in love and elope!" She laughed and twirled around, waving a satin ribbon.

Kitty looked alarmed. "But Lizzy, what would happen to me and Lydia if you *and* Jane get married?"

Elizabeth stopped Lydia by grabbing her shoulders and holding her until she no longer swayed. She then led the younger girl to the bed to sit beside Kitty.

"First, I would never elope. What a scandalous thing to do!"

Lydia shrugged and giggled. "I know, but what a lark it would be!"

Elizabeth shook her head and rolled her eyes while chuckling. "I will not leave while you two and Mary still need me. You need never fear that."

Kitty bit her lip and looked towards the door. "I would like to see you get married, it is just that..."

They could hear Mrs Bennet demanding the attention of the housekeeper, a maid—who was supposed to be assisting Mary—and Jane. Elizabeth reflected, *No doubt, Papa is in his room, grumbling about the necessity of going with us. At least he does not add to the senseless noise.*

Pushing aside her reflections, Elizabeth smiled at her sisters and touched their cheeks. "I am almost finished. Please, go help Mary. I am afraid she is alone."

The girls did as bid, and half an hour later, the five Bennets were in the carriage and on their way to Netherfield. The journey was silent, with Mrs Bennet's occasional huffing and pointedly looking away from her husband the only interruption. Elizabeth exchanged looks with Jane and Mary, who sat on the forward-facing seat with their mother. She knew that they, like her, were praying their parents would act like respectable people and not show their unhappiness to the world.

I shall not let them destroy my enjoyment of the evening. Tonight, I shall immerse myself in my surroundings and not let their behaviour vex me.

After being greeted by the Bingleys and Hursts, they walked into the ballroom, the decoration of which was lovely. The floor gleamed and candlelight bounced off cream-coloured walls. Bright flowers adorned the mantelpiece, and the chairs and benches along the walls were interspersed with tall plants. A quartet of musicians, stationed at one end of the long room, was playing a selection of Gluck's *Water Music*. Mr Bennet quickly wandered off, no doubt to find companions more to his liking, then Mrs Bennet saw her friends and left the girls, which suited Elizabeth well.

Together with Jane, Elizabeth and Mary exchanged a few words with various neighbours and people from nearby towns they only met occasionally. Elizabeth saw a number of officers—but not Mr Wickham—and people she did not recognise whom she assumed were friends of the Bingleys come from London. She looked for Mr Darcy and discovered that he stood with a group of local men and gave every appearance of being engaged in their conversation.

While dancing the second set with Mr Denny, she learnt that, in the gentleman's words, "something curious happened earlier today."

"Oh? What was that?"

"Wickham was called to a meeting with Colonel Forster. I have not seen him since."

Elizabeth wondered if Mr Darcy's letter to his cousin had had something to do with that. *I can only hope it is not a matter of Mr Darcy and his cousin using their greater influence to make Mr Wickham's life difficult for petty reasons. I must hope that Mr Darcy's dislike of him is justified. I would have to be blind not to see that there is a great deal more to the connexion than I know.*

They spoke no more about Mr Wickham.

Twice before supper, Elizabeth's pleasure was disrupted by her parents. After her dance with Mr Denny, she was speaking to an acquaintance and stood not far from Mrs Bennet and Mrs Philips. Upon hearing Mrs Bennet mention Jane and Mr Bingley, Elizabeth excused herself to go to her mother and aunt.

"Mama, please lower your voice. Mr Bingley will not like to hear himself talked—"

Mrs Bennet waved a hand as if sweeping away her daughter's words; in her other hand, she held a glass of punch. "You worry too much, Lizzy! That might have mattered in the past, but he is so enraptured with your sister that it can make no difference now. Besides, I am sure he would like to know how happy I am about the match and what sort of welcome he will get once he proposes."

Whatever my mother thinks, it was never likely that a man such as Mr Bingley would marry one of us. Behaviour such as this ensures they will not.

Mrs Bennet continued, "Mark my words, he will make his addresses anytime now, perhaps even tonight. He will make a fine son-in-law. Five thousand a year! How jealous everyone will be of my good fortune. Mr Bennet will never again dare to say anything to me about economising. Did I tell you what he said to me just yesterday, Sister? Oh, what a horrible man I married!"

Elizabeth left them. If she remained any longer, she would go mad.

During the next interval, it was Mr Bennet's turn to show the family to disadvantage. He stood with an elderly gentleman Elizabeth only vaguely recognised. She was looking for Mary, when she heard her father say, "It is a tedious way to spend an evening. Ah, there is one of my brood."

He grabbed Elizabeth's arm and tugged her to his side. After introducing her to his companion, he said, "I was just saying how little I like this sort of thing. I had much rather be at home, in my snug book room, with only the sound of turning pages and the crackle of the fire to disturb me. I suppose there is some humour in watching the young people—and some of the not so young—making fools of themselves as they chase after those of the opposite sex." He turned to Elizabeth. "Jane is not doing a very creditable job of catching Mr Bingley, despite your mother's instructions. What about you, Lizzy? Which gentleman have you decided upon? Or, should I say, which one has your mother selected for you? Dare I hope she has found someone for Mary, too, and my house will be rid of some of its excessive noise and my wallet spared the expense of having so many daughters?"

It was not the first time she had heard him attempt such a jest. Bitterness always seeped into his voice, and it left Elizabeth with the sensation that someone had reached into her and pulled out something vital—some part of her that made her lighter and happier.

She sighed. "Papa."

Mr Bennet released her arm. "Oh, go off with you. Leave me to find what pleasure I can from making sport of my neighbours."

As she walked away, she silently added, *And your family*.

Shortly after separating from him, she was stopped by Jane, who linked their arms and led her to a quiet corner.

"What is it, Lizzy? You look upset."

Elizabeth told her about the scenes with their mother and father.

"You should not take it so hard," said Jane. "I do wish they were more circumspect, but I would rather see you relax and savour every moment of tonight. Is it not a wonderful ball?"

Elizabeth forced a smile. "You are well amused, I take it?"

"I am." Jane's eyes darted around the room before she put her mouth close to Elizabeth's ear and whispered, "I have danced once with Mr Bingley, and he has asked me for the supper set. I have not forgotten your advice. I am determined to simply enjoy his company tonight without hoping— Oh, Lizzy, it is hard! I do like him. Very, very much."

"I know you do, and it is understandable; he is very amiable." Elizabeth squeezed her sister's hand, suppressing the desire to once more urge Jane towards caution.

Mr Darcy claimed his dance before supper. Elizabeth had to admit that he looked particularly handsome in his formal attire. The contrast between his snowy cravat and black jacket was elegant, and the deep green of his waistcoat shimmered and heightened the colour of his dark eyes. She had noticed him dancing with several different ladies—including Mary, for which she was particularly thankful—and talking to a number of gentlemen. She had to give him credit; it seemed he was genuine in his desire to alter the neighbourhood's opinion of him.

"Are you enjoying yourself, Miss Elizabeth?" They stood across from each other, waiting for the signal to start.

"I am. Are you?"

As they began to move through the patterns, he said, "I doubt I shall ever be able to claim that I like balls. Nevertheless, the answer to your question is yes."

She laughed. "You sound surprised."

His lips formed a soft smile. "I am. As determined as I was to practise my civility, I expected it to be a sore trial. I can easily name a half a dozen activities I would rather be occupied with this evening, but—for a ball—I find it agreeable."

"It was very kind of you to ask Mary to dance," she said.

"The pleasure was mine, I assure you."

"Speaking of Mary, do you know the gentleman she is dancing with?" Elizabeth gestured to where Mary was standing up with a soldier she did not recognise.

"Lieutenant Willis. If I remember correctly, he is the younger son of a clergyman. I found him pleasant. Quieter and more serious than many of the other officers."

She smiled her thanks for the information. When the dance put them side-by-side, she almost mentioned Mr Bingley, but a desire to relish the moment—the fine music, the company of a handsome man—kept her silent. She cursed herself for being selfish, yet it was not enough to make her hint that Mr Bingley should refrain from giving a false impression of his intentions towards Jane. Instead, she asked him how the countryside in Derbyshire compared to that in Hertfordshire. It was a subject upon which he spoke freely, and Elizabeth found watching and listening to him oddly satisfying. At the very least, she would no longer say that she disliked him. He was well-spoken, and their conversation was interesting. Now that he was making the effort, he displayed excellent manners. He was handsome, too, which made it a pleasure to look at him.

I never thought I would say this, but I think I enjoy his company.

EIGHT

Darcy was more and more intrigued by Miss Elizabeth Bennet. There was no denying that he was attracted to her looks, but it was what she did that particularly drew his attention. He saw in her someone who would understand and share his devotion to those under his care, from Georgiana to his servants, tenants, and the people in his parish in Derbyshire who depended on his charity. He so easily saw the weight of responsibility on her slender shoulders. Since he often experienced a similar burden, it was easy to recognise. He wondered that others did not do more to lighten her load. The more he saw of Mr and Mrs Bennet, the less he expected they would do anything to assist their second daughter. Miss Mary seemed too much in awe of Miss Elizabeth, and too used to being take care of, to take on any of her sister's role in their family.

Miss Bennet, on the other hand, could and should do more. I do not know if it is just Bingley's being here, but I suspect it goes beyond that. Miss Elizabeth has the sort of personality that sees a problem and seeks to fix it; Miss Bennet is less apt to admit that anything is amiss or to see unpleasantness even if directly confronted by it. Her apparent friendship with Bingley's sisters shows that.

When they had walked together just two days earlier, he had been shocked by Miss Elizabeth saying that she did not consider him a friend. Upon reflection, he understood. While he had observed her a great deal, they had not spoken much. She had also been correct when she said he had not behaved as he ought since coming to Hertfordshire. Although he had asked for her opinion, her response had perhaps been too frank, too lacking in delicacy, but she had a way about her that made him want to forgive her anything.

Forgive her anything, and give her everything.

Bingley was well on his way to forming an alliance with the Bennets, and Darcy had nothing to say on that score. Bingley could afford to make a disinterested choice. But *he* was a Darcy of Pemberley. His wife should have impeccable breeding and a substantial dowry. It was what his parents had expected of him, and his remaining family would not approve of him putting matters of affection above those of wealth and connexions.

Good God. I cannot be thinking of marriage! I admit, I should like us to be friends, especially if Bingley and Miss Bennet make a match of it. But marry Elizabeth Bennet? It is in every way impossible.

Darcy escorted her into supper and found them seats

towards the back of the room. After the first rush of eating, Bingley encouraged the ladies to provide them with music.

"Miss Mary Bennet," he said, "will you favour us with a piece?"

Miss Mary stood and glanced at Miss Elizabeth. Darcy watched as she smiled encouragingly and nodded. With that, Miss Mary went to the instrument and began to play an air by Bach.

When Miss Mary had completed the piece, Darcy asked Miss Elizabeth, "Will you play tonight?"

Miss Elizabeth shook her head. "I told Mr Bingley not to ask me. Too many comparisons are drawn between me and Mary and most of them forget that I am two years her senior. I wanted her to be the only Bennet who displayed her talents tonight."

While understanding her reasons, he was disappointed.

Miss Bingley took her place at the instrument after Miss Mary quit it. Darcy obtained several tarts for Miss Elizabeth and himself and had just taken a bite of a tangy lemon one when Mrs Bennet's shrill voice pierced his eardrums. The lady was sitting some ways away, meaning she must be speaking quite loudly. The redness of her complexion hinted that she had drunk too much of Bingley's good wine. Miss Elizabeth's face became ashen as her mother spoke, and her hand—holding a forkful of pastry six inches from her mouth—trembled.

"Yes, well, it is good that Mary has some talent at the pianoforte, I suppose," Mrs Bennet said. "She is nothing to look at and not at all good-natured, unlike my Jane. I despair of ever finding her a husband. Lizzy is no better, although she puts on such airs, as if she is superior to the rest of us. Once Jane is married to Mr Bingley, she will be able to introduce her sisters to all of his rich friends. With luck, I shall see them all married by the summer, even Mary, if I am very fortunate."

The speech was astonishing enough, but the fact that Mrs Bennet appeared to include Miss Catherine and Miss Lydia in her matrimonial scheming sickened him. Darcy looked to see what Mr Bennet would do, supposing he had witnessed his wife's display. Miss Elizabeth had also turned towards her father. Mr Bennet did nothing more than snigger and roll his eyes. Miss Elizabeth's distress seemed to worsen, and Darcy was thoroughly disgusted by both of her parents. Miss Bingley quickly finished the concerto she had started and left the instrument. Mrs Hurst stood and the two met off to the side, bent their heads together, and hid their faces with their fans. Darcy had no doubt that they were laughing at the Bennets, who they had so often disparaged in his hearing. He was as repelled by their behaviour as he was that of Mr and Mrs Bennet.

Miss Elizabeth stood and took a step as though she would go to Miss Mary, but Miss Bennet was already by their younger sister's side. Miss Elizabeth, her features impassive, turned and strode out of the room.

Darcy followed her to the terrace, although he was not certain she knew he was behind her. She stopped at the end of the pavement and covered her face with her hands. He heard a muffled sound of frustration or perhaps embarrassment, either of which would be understandable.

"Miss Elizabeth?" He kept his voice soft to avoid

alarming her. Nevertheless, she started, turned to face him, and surreptitiously wiped her cheek. He hated her parents for hurting her, to say nothing of the injury they did to their other daughters.

"Oh, Mr Darcy. I did not hear you."

She looked away from him, staring into the night, and he stepped to her side. He wanted to say something comforting but knew not what. Afraid of distressing her further, he remained silent and hoped that his presence would be enough.

"How you, how *everyone*, must despise us," she said with a sad little laugh.

"You are not to blame for how your mother and father act."

With her eyes closed and chin lowered, she made a soft sound that, to his ear, encompassed moroseness, exhaustion, and anger.

"Will you sit with me?" he asked.

There was an iron bench to the side. When she moved towards it, he shrugged out of his coat and draped it over her shoulders, and she whispered her thanks. It was too cold to remain outside for long, but he believed she needed a few minutes to regain her composure.

Darcy said, "Did I ever tell you about my aunt? She has the impression that she is the most intelligent, most accomplished, sensible person in any room, and that this gives her the right to tell everyone—be they a scullery maid, her nephews, or even her brother's wife—what they should do. Let me correct myself; not what they *should* do, what they *must* do. If people do not do her bidding quickly enough, she will repeat the demand at ever louder volumes until they do.

"When I was a child, she terrified me. I remember when we were visiting her once, she saw me and my cousin—the one who is now a colonel— playing on the lawn. We were using sticks as swords, pretending to fight some enemy or other. We were so intent on our game, and we had several dogs with us who added their barks to our battle cries, that we did not hear her approach. She said our names so loudly that both of us jumped. I almost— Well, I believe I will keep that detail to myself."

His last words had the effect he hoped. She looked at him, and while her expression still hinted at her distress, it had eased.

He continued, "One of the dogs ran away. It was my father's, and he had to go searching for it. He was furious with her."

"What did she object to?"

"Our behaviour was not dignified enough, given our birth and position in life. We both had dirt on our clothes, our hair was messy, et cetera. Mind you, the only people who would have seen us, apart from the servants, were her and our parents. When our mothers took exception to her reprimanding us, there was quite the row."

"I should imagine so."

Miss Elizabeth looked so lovely as she spoke. The moonlight made her skin and hair luminous and added a sparkle to her beautiful eyes. There was something about seeing her with his coat wrapped around her that made his fingers yearn to touch her. As it was, he struggled not to slide closer to her on the bench.

"I dread her ever being in town when I am," he admitted. "It raises the possibility of us being in company together. I am ashamed of myself when I avoid her, but she is so unpleasant and exhausting. Amongst her other demands is that I marry her daughter. She insists that it was my mother's fondest wish. My mother died before I was old enough for us to talk about such things, but I know my father did not favour the match, if only because it would make my aunt my mother-in-law."

"Is that the only objection you have to marrying your cousin?" Elizabeth asked. "You will understand me when I say that it is hard to condone a lady being overlooked because of a parent's behaviour."

"No." He shook his head to emphasise the point. "I regret to say that my cousin is too much like her mother. She seldom talks, and when she does, it is to complain about her health, demand someone does something for her—even things she could easily do herself—or say something unkind about another person, even her companion while the poor lady is sitting beside her. Truly, they are not nice."

Miss Elizabeth offered him a smile. "I thank you for telling me, Mr Darcy. I assume you did it to make me feel less wretched about the display my mother and father have made of themselves this evening."

"I will say it again, my dear Miss Elizabeth, you are not responsible for how they behave. I trust no one who has the pleasure of knowing you and your sisters will ever judge you because…" He did not know how to finish his thought without being indelicate.

"Because my mother speaks too loudly and indiscreetly, and my father chooses to make a joke of it rather than check her behaviour?" She sighed. "I am so tired of it all. For years they have— It is not only this."

She fell silent, but he sensed that she wanted, perhaps needed, to talk about it. It thrilled him that she might, with a little encouragement, confide in him. There could be no surer mark that her opinion of him had improved.

"Say what you will, Miss Elizabeth. I assure you, I shall tell no one."

She hesitated for just a moment before saying, "They argue, loudly and often. They were never well-suited, and disappointment at not having an heir—Longbourn is entailed, and a distant cousin will inherit—has made their discontent with each other all the worse."

Darcy nodded and gently urged her to continue.

"From the time I was ten or thereabouts, I remember them quarrelling. Not little disagreements, which I suppose any married couple has, but acrimonious battles —yelling that seems to shake the house, such horrible insults, and it ends with my father ignoring us all the more and my mother crying and complaining about everything." She sighed. "You mentioned that I take care of my sisters. It is because of the situation with my parents. I like to think I would have been an attentive sister whatever the circumstances, but as my parents' relationship grew worse, they neglected us girls more and more. Jane and I were old enough to understand, and we did not require so much supervision, but Mary, Kitty, and Lydia needed our help. I hate to think what they would be like now elsewhere."

"What did you do?"

She shrugged. "What had to be done. I will always do whatever I must to ensure my sisters are as happy as possible and have the futures they deserve."

That, he intuited, included protecting them from Mr and Mrs Bennet. Something in her manner left him assuming there was more to the situation than she was saying.

They were silent for about a minute until she said, "I apologise, Mr Darcy. You can have no wish to hear me complain, and I ought not to have said what I did about my father and mother."

The last thing he wanted was for her to regret confiding in him. "I have often found that it helps to express one's frustrations to another. My cousin, the one I have previously mentioned, serves that same purpose for me. He is more a brother to me than a cousin."

"You are fortunate to have him. There is only so much I can say to Jane. She is the sweetest, most good-natured person I know, and I would not see her change for anything."

"But that makes it difficult for her to understand your feelings?"

She nodded, stood, and removed his coat. "I ought to return before I am missed. I would like to talk to Mary and be sure she did not take my mother's words to heart."

He had jumped to his feet and looked down into her face. "Of course. I shall follow you in a few minutes."

With a smile that did not reach her eyes, she left him alone. He dropped back onto the bench and watched her walk away, his eyes not moving even when she was lost in the crowd of people in the ballroom. He sensed in her a loneliness that reflected what he often felt. He had responsibility—including for his sister—thrust upon him by the early death of his parents. Miss Elizabeth had assumed more responsibility than she ought to have had to bear because of the selfishness of her parents, and she had done it for the good of her sisters.

What a remarkable woman.

NINE

The following morning, Bingley went to London to see to several business matters. Darcy was awake early enough to see him off.

"I hate to go. I would not, if it was not so important." He sighed and dropped into a chair, his gaze drifting to the ceiling. Darcy suspected he was seeing something other than the gold-flecked plaster decorations. "Was not the ball wonderful? Miss Bennet was perfection. She always is—so gentle and-and caring—but last night, she was especially lovely. I have never met a lady like her."

Darcy resisted the temptation to roll his eyes. He would have, if he did not suspect Bingley's feelings were more than a passing fancy. "Do you intend to offer for her?"

Bingley jerked as though surprised by the sound of Darcy's voice. "Eh? Oh, right. Yes. I mean, absolutely."

His eyes implored Darcy, "Do you think she will accept me? She will, will she not? I think she likes me. She seems to."

"She gives every indication of returning your affection, from what I have seen." *When I have not been studying her sister, that is.*

A broad, unseeing grin covered Bingley's face. "Do you know, I believe I knew the moment I met her that I would ask her to be my wife."

He sighed loudly and dramatically enough that Darcy almost recommended he seek a role on the stage.

Scratching the back of his neck, Bingley faced Darcy and asked, "Tell me, Darcy, what is your opinion? Caroline and Louisa like Miss Bennet, yet I fear they will not be pleased. They will say I should marry a lady with connexions and a large fortune. I always thought I would, but then I met my darling—"

Darcy could not bear to hear him speak about Miss Bennet's beauty, a subject Bingley had bored him with quite enough since they came into Hertfordshire. "Only you know what will bring you happiness. Miss Bennet is an estimable woman. If you are fortunate enough to win her hand, then I shall be the first to wish you joy."

Bingley grinned. "I knew I could count on you." The hall clock chimed, and Bingley leapt to his feet. "Is that the time? I really should go. I will be back soon. A couple of days. As quickly as I can. Do you want to come with me? I know you do not long for my sisters' or Hurst's company." He screwed up his features. "But here you can ride, and it is very pretty countryside, and—"

"You will return in two or three days' time?"

Bingley nodded.

"Very good. I shall see you then."

ELIZABETH AWOKE EARLY despite the late night at the ball and an hour spent telling Kitty and Lydia about it once they returned to Longbourn. She slipped out of the house and went for a walk, enjoying how quiet and tranquil the morning was. After about a quarter of an hour, she was startled by the sound of Mr Darcy approaching on his horse. He dismounted, and they exchanged greetings.

"May I walk with you?" Mr Darcy asked.

Elizabeth kept her smile polite, but she felt like grinning. After their dance, she had decided he was not the disagreeable man she had believed him to be, and she would not object to spending more time in his company. Then, the way he had encouraged her to confide in him, his understanding and delicacy—even the way he had told her about his aunt—had made her like him. As she readied herself for bed last night, she had been worried that she had lost his respect after speaking so freely and saying such disparaging things about her parents. To see him now, showing every sign of pleasure—a quiet smile and tranquil air—left her with a sense of weightlessness that she took for relief. His opinion should not matter to her, yet it did.

Which is not something I shall think about at the moment! She would much rather enjoy his company and the opportunity to get to know him better.

They ambled aimlessly, Mr Darcy leading his large black stallion by the reins.

"How are you this morning, Miss Elizabeth? Recovered from the ball?"

She laughed. "I am very well, Mr Darcy, and assure you I am stern enough to withstand the rigours of a ball. You, on the other hand, might not be able to say the same. You look well enough, I suppose, or do I detect a lingering nervous twitch near your left eye?"

He made a deep chuckle, and this time, Elizabeth did grin. She could never like a person who would not be teased, and it was a relief to discover that Mr Darcy was not so cheerless. "You are out early this morning."

"Bingley left for town, as I believe you knew he intended to do." She nodded, and he continued, "I wished to see him off."

Elizabeth bit her lips together and listened to the rhythm of the horse's hooves clip-clopping on the hard ground while she searched for the right words. She was determined to seize this unexpected encounter to Jane's advantage. "I am surprised you did not go with him."

"Are you?"

"I have seen… It appears to me that Miss Bingley and the Hursts do not like the neighbourhood, and I know that Mr Bingley took only a short lease on Netherfield." She shrugged. "I admit, I expected all of you to depart once the ball was over."

"Did you? I cannot disagree with you regarding the ladies and Hurst, but my friend very much likes the neighbourhood—one lady in particular."

Mr Darcy had stopped walking, confusion making him furrow his brow and peer at her. A part of her knew she should remain silent, but she had to speak. She straightened her spine and reminded herself that, no matter how much Mr Darcy might despise her being so forthright, she had to protect Jane.

"You imply my sister Jane."

"I would have thought it was obvious."

"That he admires her beauty? Yes. That it means anything more than that? No."

Mr Darcy took a half-step backwards. "Wh... Do you accuse him of trifling with her affections? What could he have possibly done to lead you to such a conclusion?"

In the face of his shock, Elizabeth prevaricated. "No, nothing so— Perhaps of not realising how his manner might mislead her and others into thinking he felt more than he does. Many men have been struck by Jane's beauty, yet she remains unmarried. She has been gravely mistaken about men in the past and is too-too"—a part of her wanted to say foolish—"good to believe it could happen again."

Twin red spots covered Mr Darcy's cheeks, and his jaw was rigid. When he opened his mouth to respond, she hastened to speak before he could.

"I am not insensible to the ways of the world, Mr Darcy. My most fervent prayer is that my sisters make good marriages. I have done everything in my power for the last eight years to ensure that they are respectable and prepared to be good wives. But I also know that we have little to recommend ourselves. My parents are disgraceful; we have no fortunes, and no connexions to offer any gentleman. Men like Mr Bingley—"

He interjected, standing tall, his features hard. "I beg you will not continue. I do not know what manner of man you assume he is, but you are mistaken. To believe that all men who are wealthy are— I would not expect you, of all ladies, to hold such prejudices. My friend is an honourable gentleman. He admires your sister. He would never, *never* show her such marked favour if he were not prepared to see it to its natural conclusion."

Elizabeth's heart thudded painfully, and her legs felt weak. "Do you mean that he intends to propose to her?"

Mr Darcy gave a single curt nod. "He and I have spoken about Miss Bennet a great deal, including this morning. I assure you, a thousand times, he is very serious."

Elizabeth could only stare at him. If he were right... *Oh, Jane, have I been so mistaken? Have I injured you, of all people?*

"Why do you find that so difficult to accept?" demanded Mr Darcy. "Do you dislike Bingley, or have you seen something in him that makes you assume he could be so deceptive? I could understand you saying you believed *I* could act in such a manner, I who am adept at offending people, but not Bingley, who is open and friendly."

Almost desperate for him to understand, Elizabeth said, "Do you not see how that raised my suspicions? From almost the moment they met, he has been fixed on her. It is like the bright spark that suddenly erupts, then just as quickly fades. *That* is how I see his attachment to her. That is what I am afraid it is. When it does burn out, where does that leave my sister? With a broken heart, if not a damaged reputation. And who will be left to support her, to help her recover?"

Elizabeth flushed, realising her words sounded self-ish, but she had not intended them in such a fashion, and in Mr Darcy's presence, she felt unaccountably exhausted with her life and all its responsibilities. How would she find the fortitude to help Jane if Mr Bingley abandoned her sister, especially knowing that Jane truly had given her heart to him? It had been difficult enough after the affair with Mr Chaplin. Her voice was weak when she added, "I do not want to see her suffer."

"I do not know what I can say to convince you that you are wrong. I have known Bingley for years, and I have seen him admire other ladies. It is only natural. But —and I cannot emphasise this enough—what he feels for Miss Bennet is unlike anything he has experienced before. He told me that, from the moment they met at the assembly, he knew she was the lady he would marry. You are mistaken about him, Miss Elizabeth, entirely mistaken. You do him and your sister a disservice by clinging to the notion that he would abandon her, that she—that any of your sisters—are not good enough for a man such as Bingley. You are wrong about his character. He does not deserve your low opinion; I know he has done nothing to deserve it."

"I never said—"

Again, he interjected, "You may not have said it, but it is what your words and thoughts imply. Good morning."

With a quick bow, he turned away from her, and in an instant, was atop his horse and riding away. Elizabeth stared after him, tears pooling in her eyes.

❧

DARCY SUCCESSFULLY AVOIDED Bingley's family until dinner. At first, he was angry with Elizabeth

Bennet for thinking meanly of his friend, but—after a long ride followed by a great deal of pacing around his room—he forgave her. It behoved any lady to question a man's true intentions, and Bingley was a stranger to the neighbourhood. There were none other than his own party who could speak for him. By rights, it should be Mr Bennet who protected his daughters, but he was neglectful, and Miss Elizabeth—loyal, devoted sister that she was—had taken up the role.

She was mistaken, but if she is half the woman I believe she is, she will admit it, Darcy thought as he looked out his bedchamber window. It faced the courtyard, and he recalled the previous evening when he had anticipated her arrival. Every minute they had spent together had been delightful—to him at least—even the difficult minutes together at the end of supper, when she had been distressed by her parents' behaviour. *Dare I hope she takes my word for it?* For some reason he could not name, it would mean the world to him if she did.

By the time he saw Mrs Hurst and Miss Bingley, they were nothing short of agitated. Dinner conversation centred on everything they found disagreeable about the ball—the people, what they wore, how they spoke, danced, stood. He could not abide their ridiculous and incredibly petty speech. He attempted to ignore them and engaged Hurst in conversation, but, as usual, the man had nothing to say for himself.

In the withdrawing room, Miss Bingley and Mrs Hurst attacked him with a plan to separate Bingley and Miss Bennet. It had occurred to them that their brother was serious about the lady. Darcy was sitting on a wine-coloured armchair near the fire, a cup of tea on the table beside him and a book in his hands. The ladies perched on the footstool, and he wished he had put his feet up. *As if that would have stopped them.*

Mrs Hurst said, "Do you know what we learnt when she so conveniently fell ill and had to stay here? She has an uncle who lives in Cheapside and is in trade!"

"He lives within sight of his warehouses." Miss Bingley's tone combined triumph and disgust. "Is such a girl to be our sister-in-law?"

"You must help us, Mr Darcy. Speak to Charles; he will listen to you."

Miss Bingley leant towards him, the crystal pendant of her necklace swinging back and forth. "We must depart this place at once, join Charles in London, and convince him to give up Netherfield. The neighbourhood is without fashion or a single decent family."

Darcy's grip on the book tightened. Meeting each lady's eyes in turn, he said, "I will have no part in this." They made noises of disappointment, and he carried on. "I told your brother I would remain here until his return, and that is what I intend to do."

"But Mr Darcy," Caroline Bingley whined, "the Bennets! Not a one of them is worthy of our notice, especially not yours."

How I wish I could tell her my true opinion—that any of the Miss Bennets, Miss Elizabeth in particular, is worth a score of Miss Caroline Bingleys. Aloud, he said, "Mr Bennet is a gentleman, and I have heard that his people have held Longbourn for over one hundred years. Miss Bennet and her sisters are charming, well-mannered young ladies."

"Without fortune or connexions." Miss Bingley's lips curled in apparent anger.

Adopting a more moderate tone, Mrs Hurst said, "Miss Bennet is a sweet girl, but her sisters—"

"Miss Mary is a mouse, and as for Miss Elizabeth—"

Darcy interjected, "I find them both estimable, interesting, and kind. If your brother does not object to the Bennets' connexions, it can be nothing to you."

"Our position as a family would suffer!" Mrs Hurst argued.

It was difficult not to sneer at them. "I would hope that all of us judge others by more important measures than their wealth and who their family is." Miss Bingley and Mrs Hurst gaped at him with almost identical expressions. "If Miss Bennet and your brother truly care about each other—as I believe they do—then it would be wrong for any of us to intervene."

They argued with him, and he conceded that, since they felt so strongly about the matter, they should explain their concerns to their brother—if they were prepared to live with the consequences. He repeated, "I will have no part of it."

The ladies appeared to accept his decision, though he expected them to revisit the subject in the morning, perhaps even to present their departure as a *fait accompli*, forcing him to leave Hertfordshire when they closed up the house. As soon as they vacated the footstool, he put his feet on it and opened his book.

Staring at the page, he said to himself, *How can I leave when I cannot stop thinking about Miss Elizabeth? I must proceed with care lest I do what I warned Bingley against and raise expectations I cannot meet.*

He had to consider the duty he owed to his heritage and his family. Georgiana was foremost in his mind. But would Miss Elizabeth not be good for Georgiana? Would that not more than overcome the drawbacks of such a match? If, that was, he decided he loved her—in truth, he knew he did but was afraid of what acknowledging it would entail—and wanted her for his wife.

❧

ELIZABETH DID NOT SEE Jane for several hours after returning from her unexpected meeting with Mr Darcy. She had immediately gone to her bedchamber, sent word that she had a headache after sleeping poorly, and asked that she not be disturbed. For the next while, she sat at the window and reflected on Mr Darcy's words, Mr Bingley, and Jane. Mr Darcy had been quick to correct himself when she pointed out his errors. She owed it to him—to say nothing of her sister and Mr Bingley—to determine whether she had been wrong and, if she had, to acknowledge it.

When she went downstairs, she discovered that she had missed Charlotte's call. At the moment, she could not regret it. She did not want to talk over the ball and speculate on the meaning behind this man dancing—or failing to dance—with that lady, as Charlotte often liked to do. Jane and Mary were in the parlour sewing and chatting, and she joined them, although she could not attend to their conversation.

A half an hour later, she seized the opportunity of Mary's momentary absence to say, "Jane, I have been thinking, and I believe I was mistaken about Mr Bingley." She glanced up from her work and saw that Jane stared at her, her lips parted and eyes sparkling with hope. "I do not believe I was wrong to caution you when we first met him, but now that we know him better, I do believe him to be a good man. He would not treat you falsely."

Jane threw her work aside and sat beside Elizabeth, clutching her arm. "Oh, Lizzy. Do you truly think so?"

Elizabeth nodded. "But you just met in October. I know Mama would say that two days was a long enough acquaintance upon which to base a marriage. However, I cannot bring myself to believe that any thoughtful person would be quite so precipitous."

Jane smiled and produced a light laugh. "I do not think so either. I hope I have enough sense, even though it is a fraction of yours, not to act with so much haste, not after…and not when we live with daily proof of the dangers of choosing a marriage partner rashly. Thank you, dear, dear Lizzy."

Shaking her head, Elizabeth said, "You owe me no thanks. Allow what is between you and Mr Bingley to grow. Let us not talk about it further. Mary will be with us any moment, and I would not want to try to explain all of this to her." Only the two of them knew about Jane's escapade with Mr Chaplin and would understand why Elizabeth insisted on warning her to be cautious about whom she trusted.

Jane kissed her cheek and returned to her former seat.

TEN

Several days later, Mr Bingley and Mr Darcy called at Longbourn. Certain that Mr Darcy hated her for what she had said about his friend, Elizabeth did everything she could to delay the moment when she would have to face him.

"I wished to inform you I had returned." Mr Bingley ostensibly spoke to Mrs Bennet, though his eyes were on Jane more than her mother.

"It is very good of you to come, Mr Bingley," said Mrs Bennet. "We are all well, as you can see, my Jane especially. She hardly ever takes ill. It was such a surprise when she did last month. You were so kind to her when she was at Netherfield. Was he not, Jane?"

Standing beside her sister, Elizabeth saw their mother wink and silently encourage Jane to do something, probably flirt with Mr Bingley.

"Very kind. E-everyone was." Jane's cheeks were dusted with pink.

Seeing that Jane was too embarrassed to speak—and before Mrs Bennet could do something that added to the awkwardness of the moment—Elizabeth asked after the Hursts and Miss Bingley, being sure her eyes did not drift to Mr Darcy, who she knew was observing her. It made her tremble and feel queasy.

Mr Bingley cleared his throat. "They-they are well. Much…occupied."

Mrs Bennet ordered Mary to ring for tea, asked Mr Bingley to sit—she continued to either forget or ignore Mr Darcy's presence—and began a nonsensical speech about how busy ladies always were, that gentlemen never understood how much work went into managing a household—which Elizabeth found particularly humorous, given that her mother did very little of it—and what fine ladies Mrs Hurst and Miss Bingley were.

When at last she found courage enough to glance at Mr Darcy, he gave her a quick, small smile. Her head swam so violently that she almost fainted. It seemed impossible that he had not lost all respect for her. Her return smile was tentative, which evidently was invitation enough for him to sit beside her. Mary returned to Kitty and Lydia, who were at a table in the corner writing extracts from history books. Elizabeth reflected that Mary was becoming more and more helpful with their younger sisters. *I shall appreciate it if Jane marries Mr Bingley*.

"How have you been, Miss Elizabeth?" Mr Darcy's voice was gentle, and she felt an urge to lean into him.

"I am very well, Mr Darcy. You are pleased to have

Mr Bingley at Netherfield again, I am sure. You can see that his return is much appreciated at Longbourn."

Her eyes, which had flickered around the room as she spoke, landed on his. She read a silent question in his expression, and, with as much dignity as possible, nodded to indicate that she had believed him. Lowering her voice, she said, "You should hate me, Mr Darcy."

His features softened. "I could never do such a thing. You were protecting your sister, and we are strangers to you, without even mutual friends to assure you that we are honourable. I beg you to think no more about it and thank you for trusting me."

The look of approbation, perhaps with a touch of admiration—she told herself she had imagined the latter —on his face made Elizabeth blush.

Lowering his voice, Mr Darcy said, "I wanted to tell you, if you do not already know, that Wickham is gone. My cousin wrote to Colonel Forster. Between them, they arranged to send Wickham to another regiment whose commander is someone my cousin knows well. He has been warned about Wickham's tricks. We trust he will do everything possible to ensure Wickham does not impose himself upon anyone."

Elizabeth nodded. It sounded like an appropriate arrangement. Mr Wickham would keep his position, but —believing Mr Darcy that the man was not trustworthy —would be where he was unlikely to cause mischief.

And he is away from Mr Darcy, who will not now want to hasten his departure to avoid seeing him. She inhaled sharply, then covered her mouth and gave a small cough to cover the involuntary response. Where had that thought come from? True, she had learnt to appreciate Mr Darcy's company, but it was a diversion, and one she expected to come to an end before much longer. *After all, he has been in Hertfordshire above a month. He will want to return to his sister soon.*

Refusing to think about his imminent departure, she asked how he and the Netherfield party had occupied themselves since they last met. Once tea arrived, they were joined by the younger girls, and a lively discussion about what Kitty and Lydia had been studying—the English Civil War—broke out between them, Mr Darcy, and Elizabeth. Mary spoke to Mrs Bennet, freeing Jane and Mr Bingley to enjoy each other's company until the gentlemen left almost an hour later.

DURING AN EARLY MORNING ride at the start of December, Bingley exclaimed that he was pleased Darcy was at liberty to make a long visit. It alleviated Darcy's concern that he should at least hint that he would leave, which he was in no hurry to do. Georgiana remained with their aunt and uncle. Her letters were cheerful, and, in her own missives, his aunt assured him that Georgiana was doing very well. Darcy was obliged to join his family for Christmastide—and the Bingleys and Hursts were also expected in town by the end of the month—which left him several more weeks to enjoy the company of Elizabeth Bennet.

Mrs Hurst and Miss Bingley had decided to tell their brother that they did not approve of his intentions towards Miss Bennet. Darcy was not present for the discussion, but Bingley told him about it afterwards. The two of them were in the billiards room. Bingley paced like a caged animal as he railed about his sisters' impudence. Darcy watched, a cue stick in his hand.

"Never have I met a more unobjectionable lady! I do not care what my sisters think and told them so. I intend to marry her, Darcy; make no mistake about it. What do I care what her connexions are? The world is changing, and I can afford to marry for affection. I have no mother or father to please, not even any grand relations, such as you have. My sisters' snobbery I can easily overlook. It is not for them to tell me how to act!"

After listening to such talk for above a quarter of an hour, Darcy said, "Do you intend to propose soon?"

Bingley hesitated, causing Darcy to quirk an eyebrow.

"I would tomorrow," Bingley said at length. "Tonight, if it were not impossible."

"But?"

Bingley ran both hands through his hair. "Two things. I wish to give Miss Bennet more time to know me. While I am convinced that we will be the happiest couple in the kingdom, it is a serious business for a lady to leave her family. She must be comfortable with the idea."

When it was apparent that Bingley had become lost in pleasant reveries about Miss Bennet, Darcy prompted him to go on.

"Oh, yes, and I hope that Caroline and Louisa will take the next few weeks to grow accustomed to the idea and truly befriend Miss Bennet, show her they will welcome her as a sister, now that they understand my feelings. I will return after Twelfth Night and propose as soon as the moment is right. By the spring, I hope to be a married man. You will stand up with me upon that happy occasion, I hope?"

Darcy nodded, and Bingley grinned. "Excellent! Now, are we going to play a game or not?"

Darcy rolled his eyes. He had been ready to do just that for forty minutes or more.

❧

ELIZABETH WAS surprised and glad that Mr Darcy remained so long in the neighbourhood. In the weeks after the ball, she saw him a number of times, including while she was out walking with one or more of her sisters. He remained open and friendly despite her misstep regarding Mr Bingley, and Mr Bingley's manner towards her was not altered, leading her to conclude that Mr Darcy had not told him about their conversation. She appreciated his generosity and decided to forget her embarrassment and enjoy his company while she still had it. By mid-December, she began to anticipate seeing him whenever she left the house.

One such encounter was when she, Mary, and Lydia were on their way to Oakham Mount. It was a longish walk for the time of year, but the ground was dry, the sky was clear, and they had needed an excuse to be out of the house. Mr Darcy was alone. He dismounted and asked to join them. Lydia demanded his attention, and the two of them walked together, Elizabeth and Mary trailing behind. Elizabeth listened as he answered Lydia's questions about his horse and the stables at Pemberley with more patience than she would have thought he possessed a month earlier. After a while, Lydia bounded up to Mary, linked arms with her, and walked on, leaving Elizabeth and Mr Darcy to follow.

"You are very kind to always answer her questions," Elizabeth said.

"It is no hardship. I know you would agree that I can be reserved. It makes me appreciate someone who, like Miss Lydia, is so much the opposite. She is very bright."

She laughed. "I certainly did think you taciturn when we first met, but my opinion of you has changed. Before you ask, I will add for the better."

He chuckled. "I am relieved. I like all of your sisters. I find Miss Mary's company agreeable because I sense that she and I share a similar turn of mind, including a tendency to be too serious. Miss Catherine and Miss Bennet remind me of Georgiana."

They walked in silence for a minute. Elizabeth was tempted to ask him what he liked about her but was reluctant to know his answer. She contemplated her sisters, wondering what their futures would hold, and said a silent prayer that Jane and Kitty were faring well at Longbourn.

Mr Darcy said, "Forgive me if I am being impertinent, but you do not seem quite your usual self this morning. Are you well?"

Elizabeth took a deep breath and let her eyes roam over the brown, barren landscape. Had they not talked about her parents at the ball, she would make up an excuse, but since they had, she said, "We can usually tell when one of my parents'…louder battles is about to begin and find a way to avoid witnessing it. Such was the case this morning. It is best to leave the house, if possible, and I told Mary and Lydia we would go for a walk. Jane remained with Kitty, who has a cold. It is a trifling matter, but with Kitty, even a minor cold can settle in her lungs, if we are not careful. Coming out in this weather would do her no good."

He expressed his hope that Kitty would soon recover. She appreciated that he did not enquire further about her parents or offer trite comments about the situation. Instead, he began to speak about books, asking what she and her sisters enjoyed reading and telling her what he and his sister most liked. It was agreeable—more than agreeable—and Elizabeth began to feel that she was in very real danger of liking him too much.

He is so good to the girls. He seems to understand Mary better than most people do, certainly more than my mother and father do, and he is tolerant of Kitty's and Lydia's exuberance. Miss Darcy must find him to be the most excellent of brothers.

WHEN THEY MET at evening parties, Elizabeth more often than not found herself sitting beside Mr Darcy. This was true when, several days before he planned to leave the neighbourhood, they took dinner at the Stuarts'. Elizabeth had encouraged her mother to accept another invitation, and she, Jane, and Mary attended with the Lucases. The meal was unexceptional, and even if Elizabeth had not anticipated speaking to him, there was little else to draw her attention. Jane and Mr Bingley spoke to no one but each other, and Mary was occupied with one of the young Goulding gentlemen and Charlotte Lucas. Any amusement Elizabeth had found in watching how much Mrs Hurst and Miss Bingley disliked the local society had long since ebbed away.

She would never admit it to anyone, but she had dressed with particular care knowing she would see Mr Darcy. It was doing too much, but she could not convince herself to stop. Mr Darcy's appreciative look when he saw her had caused a fluttering in her stomach that still, almost an hour later, made it difficult to eat.

As she cut a piece of highly spiced venison into small pieces, she said, "It occurs to me that I know little about your family, apart from that you have a sister and a cousin who is a colonel."

His eyes widened and his brow arched as he regarded her. She thought that he, like her, was surprised that it was so, considering how often they had spoken. "I have a few paternal cousins, though we see each other rarely. Georgiana and I are closer to my mother's family—the Fitzwilliams, after whom I am named."

If she had heard his Christian name before, she had not remembered it. "Do you mean the Fitzwilliams of Romsley? Are you connected to them?"

Since he was chewing, he nodded, only speaking once he had swallowed. "The earl is my uncle, my mother's brother. He and my aunt have three sons, including the colonel."

Elizabeth was struck by the gulf that stood between them. *I may be a gentleman's daughter, but he is the grandson of an earl.* While she expected nothing more than friendship from Mr Darcy, it nevertheless felt like a physical blow.

Mr Darcy added, "I have little family beyond them,

other than my aunt, Lady Catherine de Bourgh. She is a widow and lives in Kent."

Elizabeth's brow furrowed, and she absently pushed her remaining dinner around her plate with her fork. "The name is familiar, but I cannot say why."

The reason did not come to her until she was with the ladies in the withdrawing room. When he joined them after remaining only a short time with the other gentlemen, the two of them and Charlotte Lucas spoke until Charlotte was called away by her mother.

"I have remembered why I know your aunt's name. As a gallant gentleman, you must now congratulate me."

He smiled, showing off a dimple on his left cheek. "Imagine I have said everything you wish to hear."

"Thank you kindly, sir. I will call on you to laugh and perhaps exclaim in wonder when I tell you that it was from my father's heir, Mr Collins. He wrote to my father this past October, and Papa shared the letter with me. In it, Mr Collins explained that he took orders at Easter and was granted a living by Lady Catherine de Bourgh." He gaped, and she inclined her head. "I understand the parsonage is adjacent to her estate. I do not remember what it is called."

He told her that it was Rosings Park, and the living must be that at Hunsford. "Dare I ask what he said of my aunt?"

"I must preface my answer by saying his letter was the most absurd thing I have read in a very long time—at once self-deprecating and egotistical and showing not an iota of sense. Please recall that I have never met the man, and our connexion is remote."

"I am prepared, Miss Elizabeth, and impatient, after

such an introduction."

"He made her sound like a saint."

He chuckled, the sound deep and warm. "Perhaps an interfering, officious saint?"

His good humour brought a grin to her face. "I am sure I could not say."

"More that you *will* not say, being the kind lady you are. Do you remember me telling you about my troublesome aunt at the ball?"

"I had forgotten. The one with the daughter she wishes you to marry?" He nodded. "Is she the one?"

When he nodded again, Elizabeth laughed in delight, after which they spent a few minutes—until Jane and Mr Bingley joined them—discussing the coincidence of his aunt and her cousin knowing each other.

Later that night, as she lay in bed staring at the fire, Elizabeth reflected with satisfaction on the evening. She had laughed, which she liked to do, and had spent most of it in Mr Darcy's company. She would miss him when he was gone, but she refused to think such melancholic thoughts until she absolutely must.

I might have said too much about him to Lydia tonight. I hope she does not think about it and mention it to Jane or Mary or Kitty.

In her heart, Elizabeth knew that her feelings for Mr Darcy were becoming something more than friendship. She did not want her sisters to discover the truth, not because they would tease her, but because...

What good comes from admitting it, to myself let alone anyone else? He will leave the neighbourhood, and I shall soon think of him only as a pleasant man who helped to make this autumn particularly memorable.

ELEVEN

Darcy rejoiced in his growing friendship with Elizabeth Bennet. It seemed that their time together at the ball, and the conversation about Bingley's intentions towards Miss Bennet, had removed a barrier between them. He felt they understood each other—and even themselves—better and believed she would say the same. As much as he had told himself that he was not certain what he wanted from Miss Elizabeth, apart from friendship, it was impossible to deny that his feelings for her went beyond those he had ever experienced before. The more he saw of her, the more they talked and he looked into her fine eyes, the more tethered to her he became. Increasingly, it was impossible to imagine life without her. How much his opinions, his very understanding of himself, had changed since first coming to Hertfordshire! He could recall attending the assembly in October and thinking that there was not a single person there, apart from those he already called friends, he wanted to know. Yet, even then, something about Miss Elizabeth had drawn him in. He might have called it boredom or curiosity that made him want to learn more about her, but it had been something far deeper than that. Now, as the date for his departure approached, he admitted there was only one course open to him.

On the twenty-first of December, he and Bingley called at Longbourn to say their farewells; they were leaving for town the next morning. Bingley devoted himself to Miss Bennet, as usual, and Darcy sat with Miss Elizabeth after spending a few minutes with the younger girls. He could have kissed Miss Mary for then taking Miss Catherine and Miss Lydia aside.

Miss Elizabeth looked particularly lovely that morning. There was nothing remarkable about her dress, although the tawny shade brought out the gold tones in her eyes. Her cheeks were rosy, and he longed to glide his fingers along them and trace the shape of her face. They sat away from the fire—a position reserved for Mrs Bennet on this cold day—on an overstuffed settee.

"What are your plans for Christmastide, Mr Darcy?" she asked.

"I shall spend it in town with my sister and the Fitzwilliams. My aunt and uncle always have a masquerade for Twelfth Night. They would not forgive me if I missed it without having a very, very good reason."

She smiled. "You will be pleased to see your sister, I am sure." He nodded. "What will you wear to the masquerade?"

Darcy recognised that Miss Elizabeth was teasing him. There was a certain twinkle in her eyes and arrangement of her lips that gave it away. If someone had told him two months ago that he would enjoy such a thing, he would have scoffed. *But that was before I knew her. I should still hate being teased by anyone else, but everything she does charms me, even something I would never tolerate from another.*

He responded, "I do not know. To be honest, I leave that decision to my aunt and valet. My aunt proposes ideas, and my valet protects my dignity by rejecting the more outlandish ones."

Miss Elizabeth laughed, and he delighted in it.

Darcy said, "And how will the Bennets mark the season?"

"My aunt and uncle will come from town."

"Your mother's brother?" If the brother were anything like Mrs Bennet, it could make Miss Elizabeth's life more difficult. He hated that she had to endure Mr and Mrs Bennet's awful behaviour; she did not need anyone to compound the problem.

She blushed and spoke quietly after a glance at Mrs Bennet. "He and his wife are excellent people—kind, sensible, intelligent—and I greatly anticipate seeing them. My sisters and I all do. My uncle has very little in common with either of his sisters."

"Knowing how discerning you are, I am sure they are estimable people." He could not help adding a silent, *Even if they are in trade.* He was not happy about the position of her family, but, when weighed against her merits, it mattered little. "Bingley will return in a few weeks. Your sister will be happy to see him, I imagine."

"You imagine correctly."

Darcy hesitated and ran his hands across his thighs before speaking. He studied her closely as he said, "Would anyone be happy to see me again, were I to return? Have I corrected the dreadful first impression I made?"

She averted her eyes, and the colour in her cheeks deepened as he had never seen it do before. Darcy would swear that her voice trembled when she said, "Yes." He wanted to jump up and shout his elation. He settled for grinning—not that he could have stopped it—as a warm sensation flooded his body.

Silently, he vowed, *I will see you again very soon. I do not believe I could stay away, not knowing you are here.* The absolute conviction that they belonged together, that they needed each other—and that their sisters needed them to form a new family—was firmly planted in his mind. Her simple word was like a drop of water that allowed his hope that she felt the same to sprout. He was determined to nurture it to fruition.

WHEN MR DARCY had asked if anyone would be happy to see him again, Elizabeth had wanted to throw herself at him and assure him she would, even should it be ten years before they saw each other again. Feeling exposed, she had looked away and only just managed to murmur her response. She told herself she made too much of his question; he was only teasing her about the way she had upbraided him before the Bingleys' ball.

That evening, she and Jane were alone in a small

room at the back of the house, sorting through goods for the baskets that would be distributed to their father's tenants and the parish's poor the next day. Jane mentioned their friends from Netherfield, saying the neighbourhood would feel their loss.

"As will you," Elizabeth said.

"You will, too, will you not? You may not care for Miss Bingley and Mrs Hurst, but I believe your opinion of Mr Darcy has improved."

"It has."

Jane was silent for a moment. "You *like* him."

Elizabeth chose to ignore the emphasis in her sister's statement. "He is amiable."

Jane's hands, which had been folding linen, slowed. "Lizzy, you were generous enough to reconsider your opinion of Mr Bingley. I wanted to return the favour. I know I said Kitty and Lydia were old enough to go into society, but I was being selfish and...hiding from the truth. You are right that they are too young. I do not want them to suffer the way we did or-or be tempted as I was. If you had not found—" She cleared her throat. "Mama could easily convince them to abandon their studies and enter society. Mary would not be able to prevent it. We never talked about what would happen if one, or both, of us wanted to marry."

Elizabeth swallowed what felt like a lump of coal in her throat. "There is no need to worry about it. I see now that you and Mr Bingley are perfectly suited. You will become Mrs Bingley and be exceedingly happy. I shall remain with the girls until they are old enough to take care of themselves." She forced a laugh. "I shall end up a spinster and rely on your charity. In exchange, I promise to undertake whatever menial tasks you ask of me."

"Lizzy, be serious!" There was unexpected heat in Jane's voice. "You must not sacrifice your happiness in such a way."

Elizabeth set aside the jar of preserves she had been holding and regarded Jane. "What am I giving up? No one has proposed or even shown an interest in marrying me."

Jane met her eye. "Mr Darcy."

Elizabeth laughed and resumed her sorting. "Mr Darcy has no such thought in mind. We are friends, that is all."

"Is it?"

Elizabeth's cheeks burned, and she hoped the dim light in the room would hide the evidence of her discomfort, which was almost acute enough to call misery. "Even if he did have tender feelings for me—which he does not—it would not matter." She shook her head. "I am resolved, Jane. I shall remain at home with our sisters, and you will marry Mr Bingley. He will return in a few weeks, and I would be very much surprised if you are not betrothed by the end of January."

Jane's hands stilled, and Elizabeth saw an expression of quiet joy on her face. Elizabeth felt something she had never imagined she would: jealousy. Jane would have her happily ever after with a man who loved her, whereas— even should Mr Darcy wish to marry her—she would have to refuse him.

Since he does not love me, and I am intelligent enough to know that men of his sort are unlikely to marry ladies like me, it does not matter. I will have the satisfaction of knowing I have acted in the best interests of my sisters. That *will be my happiness.*

 ❧

SHORTLY AFTER EPIPHANY, the Bennets received word that Mr Bingley had returned to the neighbour-hood. Mrs Hill heard it from the fishmonger, who had served the Netherfield cook earlier in the day. To Eliza-beth's chagrin, there was no other information, not even about how much fish was needed for the estate, which would give a clue as to the number of people in residence.

Even if I learnt there were two or three or more people there, it would not tell me what I most want to know. Oh, enough! Mr Darcy is with his sister, in town or at his estate, or-or— It does not matter!

She was standing at the window in her bedchamber, alone for the moment, having come to fetch a woollen wrap. Pulling it more closely around her shoulders, she stared at the leafless trees through the frost on the glass and willed herself to stop thinking about Mr Darcy. Unexpectedly, she had heard a great deal about him when the Gardiners visited for Yuletide. Elizabeth had known that Mrs Gardiner had spent some years of her childhood in Derbyshire, but she rarely spoke about it since it had been during that time when her parents and brother had died. In December, she discovered that her aunt had resided just a few miles from Pemberley and knew a great deal about the Darcys, all of which she was pleased to share. It made Elizabeth miss him in a manner she knew was both inappropriate and hopeless.

And destructive of my peace. It is enough that Mr Bingley has returned. I am very glad that I was wrong about him and that Mr Darcy helped me see that I was misjudging him. Jane will be happy, and it will be a good thing for our sisters. Jane will sometimes have them with her. If Jane and Mr Bingley go to town this spring, they might have Mary with them for a few weeks. The exposure to more society would do her good.

Returning to the parlour, Elizabeth discovered Mrs Bennet pacing in front of the fire, gesturing wildly, and talking about Mr Bingley. Kitty and Lydia sat together at the worktable, their heads bent low, ignoring Mrs Bennet's antics. Mary sat on a chair, her arms crossed over her chest, watching their mother through narrowed eyes. Jane was closest to Mrs Bennet. With her hands clasped in her lap and her expression showing nothing, she looked calm, but Elizabeth knew she was distressed.

"I am greatly vexed that he did not propose before going away," Mrs Bennet said. "But that does not matter now. He has returned. I shall invite him to a family dinner where we will contrive a way to leave him alone with Jane." She stopped moving, faced her eldest daughter, and pointed a finger at her. "You will encourage him. Show him that you long to be his wife. I know just what you should do."

As her mother talked about looks and touches, Elizabeth regarded Jane. There was a subtle tightening around her mouth, and her knuckles were white. When their eyes met, Elizabeth shook her head just enough to indicate that she would intervene and disrupt Mrs Bennet's machinations.

Mrs Bennet dropped into a chair and wiped her nose with a linen handkerchief. "One way or another, I will get your father to call on him at once and-and make him see that we quite consider him part of the family already. He *has* to make you an offer."

Jane exclaimed, "Mama!"

Elizabeth bit her tongue to control the temptation to tell her mother how outrageous the notion was. Mrs Bennet waved away Jane's objection. To Elizabeth's relief —and no doubt that of her sisters—their mother then left the room to find Mrs Hill and begin planning for a not-so-simple family dinner to which the person she most desired to impress had not yet been invited.

Elizabeth went to Jane and squeezed her shoulder. Jane produced a weak smile and took a deep breath, which seemed to restore the greater part of her equanimity. Seeing that Kitty and Lydia were well—they looked at her with humorous grimaces—Elizabeth sat beside Mary and took her hand. Mary's expression was stern, and anxiety for her made Elizabeth nibble her lower lip as she contemplated what to do to help her sister.

Perhaps I am being fanciful, but she does seem to feel the strain of living in such an atmosphere more than Kitty and Lydia do.

Elizabeth felt the loss of her aunt and uncle's company. Mr and Mrs Gardiner injected an air of calm and sense to Longbourn. It was a balm when they were there, but left Elizabeth bereft once they were gone. Her parents had behaved reasonably well when the Gardiners were in the house, but soon after their departure, the couple had another of their arguments. The sounds of violence had been like knives in Elizabeth's ears. Elizabeth and her sisters had scurried to the sanctuary of Jane and Kitty's bedchamber, the weather outside being too cold and icy to permit that avenue of escape. Kitty had wept uncontrollably, and it was all Elizabeth could do to prevent Lydia from intervening in the battle.

We cannot go on like this. Something has to change soon.

TWELVE

Darcy had hinted his way back to Netherfield. He had enjoyed seeing his family at the Festive Season but found that his thoughts were often with Elizabeth Bennet. He could not deny that he loved her with the sort of feeling and certainty that novelists and romantics dreamt of—not that he had ever considered himself romantic. When he saw Bingley at the start of the year, Darcy spoke about his wish to remove from town but not having the time to go to Derbyshire. He had cited some vague excuse about business and family. Bingley practically begged him to accompany him to Hertfordshire.

Darcy's purpose in returning was simple: to convince Miss Elizabeth to marry him. While in town, he told his cousins about her, seeking to gain their support for his choice of wife. They vowed to speak on his behalf when he broke the happy news to the earl and countess.

Supposing, Darcy reminded them and himself, his suit was successful.

He talked to Georgiana about Miss Elizabeth and her sisters without sharing his hopes for the future. Should he find Miss Elizabeth's manner altered upon his return, should she be unwilling to leave Longbourn, he did not want the added misery of seeing his beloved Georgiana disappointed.

"They sound like delightful girls."

Darcy detected a wistfulness in her expression and asked, "Would you like to meet them?"

When she nodded, he had immediately asked Georgiana if she would join him in Hertfordshire, and she had readily agreed. Her companion, Mrs Annesley, accompanied them. Miss Bingley and the Hursts did not. When Bingley's sisters had renewed their efforts to convince him to give up Miss Bennet, he had separated himself from them until they learnt to accept his decisions.

Once at Netherfield, impatience drove Darcy to embark on another round of hinting, this time to convince Bingley to call on the Bennets as soon as possible, regardless of the work his steward insisted needed doing. Since Bingley was anxious to see Miss Bennet, he declared that he would go to Longbourn the morning after their arrival. Darcy was invited to go with him and accepted almost before the words were out of Bingley's mouth.

When he, Bingley, and Georgiana were shown into the Bennets' withdrawing room, his eyes sought Miss Elizabeth. There was pleasure and curiosity on her face as she looked between him and Georgiana, along with a healthy dollop of surprise, which he had not expected.

I should have, he told himself. *We only truly began to be friends at the ball.* She had had no warm feelings towards him before then and may even have disliked him.

He saw how glad Miss Bennet and Bingley were to see each other again. Bingley had every reason to suppose Miss Bennet would welcome his proposal, whereas Darcy could not say the same about Miss Elizabeth. If she had thought it unlikely that a gentleman in Bingley's position could have serious intentions towards one of her sisters, she would find it even more difficult to believe that he could. *I am certain she likes me, and I shall use the next weeks to build on that, to let her know Georgiana and realise how happy we would all be as one family.*

He introduced Georgiana to Mrs Bennet and her daughters and felt like embracing Elizabeth when she offered Georgiana—and him—a warm smile. As Mrs Bennet's shrill voice filled the room, Miss Elizabeth gestured for them to sit.

"Oh, Mr Bingley, how glad we are to see you again! You promised to return, but you never know what may happen. We would have been very sorry had we never seen you again. Is that not so, Jane? Your dear sisters remained in town? What a pity! Such elegant ladies and so fond of my Jane. Come, Mr Bingley, you sit just here." In a hiss Darcy supposed she thought no one but her eldest child would hear, she said, "Jane," and pointed to the place next to Bingley on a floral-patterned sofa. "So kind of you to bring Miss Darcy, too. We are very honoured, I assure you."

She ordered Miss Mary to ring for tea, then set about

promoting a conversation between Miss Bennet and Bingley, while at the same time preventing it by refusing to be quiet herself. Darcy was happy to be ignored by Mrs Bennet for the moment.

Eventually, she will realise that another one of her daughters has an admirer, he thought. *Let us hope it is not very soon.*

Miss Catherine and Miss Lydia sat with him, Georgiana, and Miss Elizabeth. Darcy gave the two girls credit for trying to engage Georgiana in conversation, but their liveliness was too much for her. Her responses to their questions were brief and offered at little more than a whisper. Seeing how concerned Miss Elizabeth was, he met her eye and gave a gentle shake of his head. He wished he could tell her of his conviction that, with a little exposure, the three girls would be the best of friends. Indeed, he was counting on it.

The tea things were brought in, and with subtle eye and finger gestures, Miss Elizabeth directed her sisters to leave them. Miss Catherine stood and made up an excuse that fooled no one, especially since her ears turned bright red as she spoke. Miss Lydia rolled her eyes, grabbed her sister's arm, and pulled her towards their mother. Soon, Mrs Bennet was occupied by them and Miss Mary, leaving Bingley and Miss Bennet to themselves and Darcy with the two ladies he most wished to love each other.

"Miss Darcy," Miss Elizabeth said, "I am so pleased to meet you. How was your journey from town?"

Georgiana glanced at him, and he produced an encouraging smile.

"F-f-fine, thank you." A maid had served them tea, and Georgiana stared at the cup she clutched in her lap.

"I am very glad to hear that. At this time of the year, you never know what the roads will be like. Have you ever been to Hertfordshire before?"

This question was followed by others that Darcy would best describe as soft—what were her favourite music and books, did she have a cat or dog, and the like. He had the pleasure of seeing Georgiana relax to the point that she exhibited no sign of alarm when Miss Mary, yet another new person for her to meet that day, joined them.

Miss Elizabeth said, "Mary, I have discovered that Miss Darcy is passionate about music, just as you are."

With that introduction, the two girls were soon engaged in their own quiet conversation, at last giving Darcy the chance to talk to Miss Elizabeth.

She opened her mouth, her eyebrows pulled together just a touch, but failed to speak for a moment, leaving him to think that the question she subsequently posed was not what she had originally intended to say. "You brought your sister?"

"When I resolved to return with Bingley, I asked her if she would like to come with us. I knew she would enjoy the company of you and your sisters. We have several male cousins, but no ladies other than the one I have mentioned, and she is no companion for Georgiana. It would be good for her to know more young ladies."

Miss Elizabeth quirked an eyebrow. "I understand they are at least as common in town as they are in Hertfordshire."

He dipped his chin in acknowledgement. "I suppose I would counter and say that it is the…quality of young lady." He held up a hand to ward off her retort. "I do not say that there are not fine girls in London, and Georgiana has a few acquaintances from when she was at school. She does not make friends easily. I believe that spending time with you," he left the slightest of pauses before continuing, "and your sisters would help her overcome her shyness, become more comfortable in society." Darcy hoped that his meaning was clear. The lovely dusting of pink that covered her fair skin, and the way her eyes darted back and forth as if she could not hold his gaze, suggested that it was.

"I-I would be delighted to spend time with her while you are in the neighbourhood. I am sure my sisters would be, too."

"Thank you." He mentioned that Georgiana's companion had travelled with them, and they considered possible amusements.

By the time Darcy, Georgiana, and Bingley departed a short while later, he felt very hopeful that, before too long, he would have achieved his heart's desire.

❧

BY ARRANGEMENT, the Bennet sisters spent the morning with Miss Darcy at Netherfield Park two days later. Mr Darcy sent his coach to Longbourn for the ladies so that there would be no inconvenience to Mr and Mrs Bennet. Lydia and Kitty exclaimed over the carriage's fineness, and Elizabeth agreed. It was wonderful, from the gleaming exterior with the Darcy crest emblazoned on each door, to the comfortable brocade squabs and abundance of rugs and hot bricks waiting for them, even though the trip was short.

Seeing Mr Darcy appear at Longbourn with Mr Bingley had made Elizabeth feel reinvigorated; she could hardly stop herself from grinning like a fool. That he had brought his sister with him was a shock, but she was gratified that he thought well enough of her sisters to want Miss Darcy to meet them. His implication that he was particularly interested in *her* spending time with Miss Darcy had made her heart thump, but she refused to consider why he might want it.

Now, in Mr Bingley's cheerful morning room, with the weak winter sun shining through the windows and the fire valiantly battling every draught, the company had settled in for a friendly visit. Miss Darcy, Mary, Kitty, and Lydia sat at a table playing casino. Lydia had a way of making any game more boisterous than it needed to be, and Kitty was always her accomplice. To Elizabeth's relief, Miss Darcy smiled and giggled, albeit softly. Jane sat with Mr Bingley on a sofa. Elizabeth and Mr Darcy were similarly situated far enough away that both couples could enjoy private conversation. Mrs Annesley, a kindly, middle-aged widow of a vicar, sat in a corner on her own, reading a book and looking up occasionally.

Elizabeth and Mr Darcy talked about their Christmastide doings. She told him about Mrs Gardiner's having lived in Lambton, "which she said was a charming town. I believe her descriptions of Derbyshire were even more complimentary than your own."

"It is a beautiful county. Did you not previously know that your aunt had lived there?"

"I did not know exactly where or that it was so close to your estate. She does not often talk about that period of her life, which was marked by great personal loss."

"I am very sorry to hear that. I take it she has not visited Derbyshire since then. Do you think she would object to returning?"

She regarded him for a minute, not feeling certain she knew what he was asking. Would Mrs Gardiner travel to Derbyshire if, for instance, Elizabeth lived— *For pity's sake, Lizzy!*

She forced her features into a disinterested expression but found she could not maintain it for more than a few seconds. "I cannot say. Will you tell me about your aunt's Twelfth Night masquerade? What did you wear? Did you dance or stand in the corner, counting the minutes until you could depart?"

"I behaved myself very well, I assure you. I own I did not dance every set, but I managed half, I believe, and spoke to any number of people. My aunt had no complaints about my behaviour."

"And your costume?"

He hung his head and covered his eyes with one hand, which made her lips twitch. She demanded an answer.

"So that you can tease me even more?" he said.

"Exactly so! I shall not give way until you tell me."

He smiled at her in that fashion she both longed to see and wished he would never do again. It made her want things she should not.

"Very well, but only for you would I revisit it. I was Mercury."

She furrowed her brow as she tried to imagine what he had looked like. "Was he not associated with tricks and thieves? Were your aunt and valet daring to suggest a less-than-flattering aspect to your character?" She had to bite her lips together so that she would not laugh.

He narrowed his eyes as he responded, his voice flat, though Elizabeth could see that he was not truly annoyed. "He was also the god of communication and eloquence. I believe my aunt hoped that donning the costume of Mercury would imbue me with those characteristics. Needless to say, it did not work. And I shall pay more attention to what she and my valet are planning in the future."

Elizabeth could no longer hide her mirth. She laughed, and after a moment, so did Mr Darcy.

"In truth," he admitted, "the evening met my expectations. I did not dislike it, but, as you know, balls, indeed large parties of any sort, are not things I shall ever truly enjoy." After a pause, he added, "I believe you would have liked it—the spectacle, the people, and music. I would like to see it through your eyes. Perhaps then I would think better of these events."

It felt like flattery, and Elizabeth did not know what to say in response. Fortunately, refreshments were brought in, and she could occupy herself in choosing from amongst the cold meats and breads and ensuring Kitty ate more than sweets.

Some time later, when Jane signalled that it was time for them to leave, no one's regrets were louder than Mr Bingley's, although they had been at Netherfield above five hours. Mr Darcy gave Elizabeth such an intense look that it seemed to run through her, straight to her heart. She yearned to reach her hands towards him.

You are playing a dangerous game indulging in such

fantasies, Lizzy, she told herself. *You would do well to recall that he is not for you.*

Miss Darcy said, "I-I hope to see you all again soon."

Forcing her eyes away from Mr Darcy, Elizabeth replied, "And so you shall. I know I speak for my sisters when I say that we have had a lovely day. Thank you."

Sitting beside Mary on the way back to Longbourn, Elizabeth looked out of the window at the passing landscape. She heard her sisters chattering but could not make out the words. She began to believe it would do her an awful lot of good if Mr Darcy would go away again.

MRS BENNET'S family dinner was two days later. Miss Darcy joined them, as did Kitty and Lydia, since only the Bennets and Netherfield party were present. It went off as well as could be expected. Mr Bennet's sardonic tone alarmed Miss Darcy, as did Mrs Bennet's periodic attentions to her, asking impolite questions and lamenting that, like her youngest two, Miss Darcy was not yet out.

"I have tried to convince Kitty and Lydia that they are old enough—gentlemen do like the company of lively young girls—but they absolutely refuse. Why, at their ages, nothing could keep me from a dance or card party." Mrs Bennet sighed and looked into the corner for a moment, lost in her memories. "Lydia is such a pretty girl. So like me at her age. I should like everyone to see her. I do not know why they are so stubborn about it, but I know Lizzy is to blame."

Jane interjected, "Mama, did you know that Mr Jones

has told old Mr Mill that he should remove to Bath for the winter so that he can take the waters? Do you think he will?" Mr Mill's battle with gout was well known in the neighbourhood, and Mrs Bennet was sure to have a great deal to say about it, even if none of it was new or interesting. Elizabeth was grateful; she had no wish to listen to her mother harangue her—or Kitty and Lydia— about the girls entering society yet again, especially with the Darcys present.

After they ate, Mr Bennet retreated to his library. Although he asked Mr Darcy and Mr Bingley to join him for a drink, 'if you like', they declined the lukewarm invitation and went into the withdrawing room with the ladies. Elizabeth spoke about music with Mary and Miss Darcy, while Mr Darcy sat with Kitty and Lydia. Mrs Bennet moved between them and Jane and Mr Bingley. She was her usual self, but, other than a few uncomplimentary things about Mr Bennet, said nothing too outrageous. Elizabeth had little opportunity to speak to Mr Darcy alone. Nevertheless, the evening was amusing.

In their room later that night, Lydia said, "Lizzy, do you like Miss Darcy?"

"Very much." Elizabeth was sitting at the oak dressing table, brushing her hair, and looked at Lydia's reflection in the mirror. Her sister sat on the bed, her legs swinging. "Do you?"

Lydia nodded. "She is very quiet and reminds me of Mary in that way, but she likes to play games and knows a great deal about all manner of things. We have read some of the same novels and talked about it for ages when we were at Netherfield. I am not even the tiniest bit jealous that she has such lovely clothes, which I was glad to discover."

"And I am glad to know it." Elizabeth plaited her hair and turned to face Lydia. "I am happy Mr Darcy brought her with him, if for no other reason than it provides a distraction for you and Kitty. I know it is not easy to always be at home."

Lydia shrugged. "Do you think Mr Darcy will ask you—"

Before her sister could finish the question, she said, "I would not presume to guess what he will or will not do. I am tired, Lydia. Would you mind terribly if we went to sleep?"

Lydia agreed, and soon they were beneath the blankets and the candles were extinguished.

Elizabeth lay awake long into the night.

THIRTEEN

Three months to the day they first met, Jane and Mr Bingley became engaged. He proposed during a walk in the grounds at Netherfield, when the Bennet sisters were once again visiting with Miss Darcy. Jane announced the news as soon as they were together in the morning room, saying that she could not keep the joyous tidings from her dearest sisters. They were sworn to secrecy until Mr Bingley had the opportunity to speak to Mr Bennet, although there was no doubt he would grant his permission.

I will be surprised if he bothers to look up from his book when Mr Bingley asks him, Elizabeth thought. *I must convince him to act pleased for Jane's sake. He ought to be happy. Jane is overjoyed, Mr Bingley is a wonderful man, and her future is secured.*

Later that day, Jane and Elizabeth took a few minutes to have a private conversation and walked on the terrace.

Elizabeth wanted to assure Jane that she was very happy for her.

Jane smiled and clasped her hand. "Last autumn, you were right to caution me. When Mr Bingley and I first met, I told myself that he was the perfect gentleman, and that was the end of it."

"I would not call him perfect, but he is all that is good. You have chosen wisely, Jane."

Her sister blushed. "I believe I have, but I *was* careless with my behaviour and my heart. With my history, knowing I can so seldom bring myself to think ill of anyone…"

Elizabeth squeezed her hand but said nothing. She was ready to be done with *that* subject forever. She did not like to recall her past mistakes, except in so far as what she could learn from them to become a better person. In this matter, knowing how close she had come to ruining Jane's happiness—for surely Mr Bingley would have withdrawn if Jane treated him with indifference or took to avoiding him—made Elizabeth's stomach churn.

The ladies stopped walking and faced each other. Jane said, "Thank you, Lizzy, for *everything* you have done for me. I pray that one day, you will know my present happiness."

Elizabeth accepted this with a smile, pushing aside the certainty that what lay ahead of her was heartbreak, which she would have to bear alone.

Mr Bingley spoke to Mr Bennet the next day, and Jane informed Mrs Bennet that afternoon. Only the family was at Longbourn when Jane followed their mother to her dressing room before dinner and made the disclosure. Elizabeth, in the parlour with Mary, Kitty, and Lydia, was certain she felt the house shake when her mother screeched in delight. Later, in between bites of chicken and potatoes, Mr Bennet managed a very creditable congratulations to his eldest daughter.

"You are a good girl, Jane. I am sure you will be very happy," he said.

"Oh, yes, indeed," Mrs Bennet said. "He has five thousand a year, or near enough. Just think of it! My daughter—the mistress of Netherfield! Never again will I have to worry about what will happen to me when your father dies and leaves me destitute."

Mr Bennet produced a loud, heavy sigh, and Elizabeth saw him roll his eyes before lifting his glass to his lips and draining its contents. The tightness in her neck and shoulders—an inevitability when her parents were in the same room—lessened a little when he did not respond.

"And, you know," her mother continued, "once they are married, Jane will take you girls to town with her and introduce you to Mr Bingley's rich friends. Very likely, he will promote you to them. You are all prettier than Miss Bingley—even you, Mary—and he will not want to be responsible for all of you. He has ample inducement to see you married as quickly as possible."

"Mama!" a visibly shocked Jane cried.

Elizabeth left Jane to convince their mother that such schemes would never come to pass. Her father entered the fray, but his comments to his wife were less kind and only provoked Mrs Bennet. While they debated the matter, Elizabeth regarded her sisters. Mary had stopped eating. Her cheeks were pink, and she stared at her plate. Kitty watched her parents, her eyes round and complexion white. Lydia met Elizabeth's eyes and huffed. When it looked like she was going to speak, Elizabeth shook her head; it would do no good to try to stop their parents' bickering. She surreptitiously gestured to Kitty, who sat next to Lydia. Lydia understood her meaning and bent her head to whisper to Kitty, whose agitation soon began to ease, if only slightly.

Such selfish people never should have been parents, Elizabeth reflected.

After five minutes, Mr Bennet threw his napkin on the table, stood, picked up his dinner plate, and left the room. Elizabeth was glad to see him go. The ladies were silent for almost ten minutes before Elizabeth judged it safe to introduce a new topic. She was sure to choose one dull enough to cause no discomfort except fatigue.

BY THE END OF JANUARY, Elizabeth and her sisters had spent almost a dozen mornings with Miss Darcy, her brother, and Mr Bingley. They met at Netherfield, twice at Longbourn when Mrs Bennet insisted, and after planning to go walking in the neighbourhood. They went into Meryton together once. Mr Darcy had proposed it, knowing it was a favourite pastime of the Bennet sisters. There, they showed Miss Darcy the shops they liked best and took refreshments at the inn.

Elizabeth liked Miss Darcy more and more and was delighted to see her become friends with Mary, Kitty, and Lydia. It was what Mr Darcy had wanted, and Elizabeth hoped the young woman would take a new confidence with her when she and her brother left Hertfordshire. Elizabeth dreaded the day of their departure. She did not know what Mr Darcy's plans were, but assumed they would not remain much longer. She was afraid to ask him, certain her face would betray how devastated she would be when the separation came. Trying to get the information out of Mr Bingley did no good. He either did not understand her subtle enquiries or did not know himself how long the Darcys intended to stay at Netherfield.

I have only myself to blame for my hurt feelings, Elizabeth reprimanded herself many times. *I have allowed myself to develop a* tendre *for him and become attached to Miss Darcy. Stupid girl!*

Her sisters liked to talk about the Darcys. When the subject was Mr Darcy, Elizabeth refused to participate. When they discussed Miss Darcy, Elizabeth was happy to agree that she was in all ways delightful. Kitty and Lydia were full of praise for her—everything from her taste in books to her muff to how she wore her hair or took her tea. Mary, too, liked Miss Darcy, though she spoke more about her good sense and love of music.

❧

DARCY HAD every reason to be optimistic. He was enjoying his time in Hertfordshire and believed that Miss Elizabeth cared about him, perhaps even loved him as he did her. The way she looked at him, their eyes locked on each other's as they spoke, her moments of shyness when her cheeks grew rosy, her smile when they greeted each other. He rejoiced to see her befriend Georgiana, and it was apparent that, even after just a few weeks amongst the Bennet sisters, Georgiana was improved in spirits and confidence.

When he asked his sister for her impressions of them, she said, "I like them all very much, Brother. I have not spent much time with Miss Bennet, but I think —I hope—the others would consider me a friend."

"I am sure they do, Georgiana."

She bit her lip and nodded. "Miss Mary knows a great deal about music, even though she has only infrequently had a master. Miss Catherine and Miss Lydia are very amusing companions. I could not imagine nicer girls."

They were sitting in a small, cosy parlour Bingley had set aside for Georgiana's private use, and Darcy took her hand in his. He could not stop himself from saying, "You have not mentioned Miss Elizabeth. What is your opinion of her?"

His sister turned her large eyes to his. "Oh, Miss Elizabeth. She is everything that an older sister should be. She is so kind and caring. Miss Lydia said that, without her, she thinks she would be ignorant, silly, and vain. I cannot imagine *that*, but she insists it is true. Miss Mary said that Miss Elizabeth has spent years ensuring they were properly educated and taught what they need to know to be proper young ladies. I do not understand why she had to do it. They do have a mother."

Darcy patted her hand. "It is difficult to fathom why the task should fall to the older sisters to care for the younger, but I believe it says a great deal about Miss Elizabeth and Miss Bennet that they would undertake the responsibility." He knew that Miss Elizabeth would not like her sister's contributions to be overlooked, but from what he had witnessed since the autumn, she was the instigator of and force behind their scheme to step into the roles their parents ought to have played.

They were silent for a moment, and Darcy's thoughts drifted to Miss Elizabeth. Georgiana's next words were quiet and tentative.

"Fitzwilliam, I am glad you brought me to Netherfield so that I could meet her and her sisters. Do...do you hope that...?"

Darcy nodded, stood, and walked around the room.

After a minute or two, Georgiana said, "I am glad."

Turning to face her, he said, "I have yet to ask, and she has yet to say yes. There is a matter we should discuss, however. I would have you know my plans since they will affect you."

A FEW DAYS LATER, Darcy was walking beside Miss Elizabeth. Georgiana and Miss Lydia were some ways ahead of them, their arms linked, and heads bent together. The four of them were going to Meryton. Bingley and the other Bennet girls had remained at Longbourn.

"I am pleased to see how well they get along," Darcy said. "As I told you, Georgiana does not easily make friends, and to see her so at ease with your sisters is gratifying."

"She is a lovely girl. We all like her very much, and, as much as you are glad for your sister's sake that she has found friends, I am glad for my sisters. Even after so short a time, I can see that knowing her has had an influence on Mary, Kitty, and Lydia. I would say the same of Jane, but she is too much occupied with Mr Bingley to notice anything or anyone else." She chuckled.

He, too, laughed. "Bingley can be quite the bore when we are alone at Netherfield. All he talks about is Miss Bennet. I am very happy for them."

"As am I."

Darcy glanced at her. She watched their sisters and wore a smile that seemed somewhat pensive, even a touch sad. His heart began to race, and he clasped his hands behind his back. "You will miss her when she is married."

"I shall, although since she will be settled close by, at least for now, it seems nonsensical."

Forcing steadiness into his voice, he asked, "Would you consider leaving the neighbourhood?"

Her steps faltered, and he had to wait for her response. Despite the cold winter weather, he felt heated.

"I...do not anticipate having the opportunity to go anywhere."

Darcy kept his eyes on the horizon. The road dipped in fifty feet, and apart from the coats and hats Georgiana and Miss Lydia wore, all he saw was grey with the occasional green of a pine or fir tree. He swallowed heavily. "I thought, hoped, you might consent to come to Derbyshire."

He stopped walking and touched her arm so that she, too, would remain still. Stepping in front of her, he took in her expression. He could not easily interpret it; it seemed a mix of anticipation, dread, and hope. Her lips, which looked soft and enticing, were parted.

"Miss Elizabeth, you must know, I must tell you...I love you. I admire you, esteem you, respect you. Each moment we spend together is dear to me. I-I can think of a thousand words to explain how much you have come to mean to me, yet none of them suffice. Please, say you will do me the honour of being my wife."

She pressed her eyes closed, and Darcy was surprised and dismayed to see two tears slide down her cheeks. She lowered her chin, and her head began to shake from side to side. "Please, Mr Darcy, do not—" Her voice was thick when she added, "I cannot. My sisters...I cannot leave them."

She made a sound that was like a muffled sob. It reassured him, even though he hated causing her distress.

"Is that your only objection?" Caught between expectation and fear, he found it difficult to breathe. "You are concerned for your younger sisters' welfare?"

Still refusing to look at him, she nodded. "I know you cannot understand my reasons; no one can, really. But they *need* me. I am so afraid of what would become of them if I—"

Darcy grasped her hands, knowing everything he most wanted was almost his. She met his eyes, and he drew in a deep lungful of air and grinned. "I *do* understand," he assured her. "If your reason for refusing me is only because of your need to take care of your sisters, then you might as well say yes."

"I...I... What are you saying?"

"I have it all arranged. I spoke to Bingley about it the other day. Miss Mary will make her home with him and your sister. I will convince your father to allow Miss Catherine and Miss Lydia to remove to Pemberley with us. They will have the benefit of Mrs Annesley and any masters they need, in addition to your company. Georgiana, as you know, continues her studies."

She furrowed her brow. "You are not serious. My mother will never agree."

He thought it telling that she did not say her father would refuse his permission. "She would not like to have them prepared to come out in town with my sister? I think she will. And I know it will do all three of them good to have each other. As selfish as I am, I admit it will especially benefit Georgiana. You cannot imagine the change I see in her after just a few weeks. You love your sisters; I love my sister. I have no doubt you will grow to love Georgiana, just as I will grow to love Miss Catherine and Miss Lydia. Miss Mary, too, for I anticipate she will stay with us sometimes. Most of all, my dearest Elizabeth, I love you, and I cannot think of anything that I have ever wanted more than I want you to be my wife. I promise that I will do everything in my power to be the best husband and brother and, God willing, father possible. We—you, our sisters, our children, me—shall be a very happy bunch."

A hand covered her mouth, and she took a few shallow breaths. He could tell she was grinning by the tiny lines at the corner of her eyes. She nodded, removed

her hand, and said, "If you can convince my parents—
oh, how I pray you can!—then yes, a thousand times,
yes. I, oh, I do love you."

Without pausing to make sure no one would see,
Darcy swept her up in an embrace and kissed her.

FOURTEEN

Later that day, an hour after the family retired for the night, Elizabeth took Lydia's hand and led her out of their bedchamber. She held a finger to her lips to tell Lydia to remain silent. After tapping lightly on Mary's door and waving to her to join them, the three sisters went to the room shared by Jane and Kitty.

"Lizzy?" Jane asked when they entered.

Elizabeth stood with her back to the closed door. "I must talk to my sisters. We have a very important decision to make, girls."

The five of them found places to sit—Lydia and Kitty on the bed, leaning against the headboard, Jane in front of them, her legs folded by her side, Mary on the room's sole chair, and Elizabeth on the dressing table which, fortunately, was sturdy enough to bear her weight. Elizabeth could hardly believe she was about to tell them that

Mr Darcy had asked her to marry him. She was an odd mixture of elated and terrified. The promise of being his wife made her head swim and her feet long to dance. But if her sisters objected to leaving Longbourn, or if he could not convince her parents to agree, her dream would turn into a nightmare.

"Mr Darcy proposed," she announced.

Cries of congratulations and joy were followed by hushed ones to be quieter. It would not do to disturb Mr and Mrs Bennet.

Jane said, "I am so happy for you, Lizzy."

"You *did* accept, did you not?" Lydia asked.

Mary said, "Please say you did. I have believed for weeks that he loves you, and he is such a good man."

Elizabeth nodded. "He is the best of men. I did say yes, but only if it means none of you are left behind." She told them about his scheme. "Did you know, Jane?"

"Yes and no. After Mr Bingley proposed, I told him… how difficult it can be at home."

Whereas I told Fitzwilliam about Mama and Papa last autumn, reflected Elizabeth.

Jane continued, "He assured me that all of you would be welcomed to live with us. Yesterday, he hinted that he had some idea in mind and promised that everything would work out for the best for all of us, but he would not explain. Mr Darcy must have talked to him about it. I think it is a good plan. What are your thoughts?"

Elizabeth looked at each of her younger sisters in turn. "I would like to hear what the three of you think."

"Leave Longbourn?" Kitty's forehead was wrinkled, and she glanced at the others as though wanting to know what they would say.

"We would visit," Elizabeth reassured her, "and Mama and Papa could come to Derbyshire."

Lydia said, "I would rather be with Lizzy and Mr and Miss Darcy than with them."

"What about Jane and Mary?" asked Kitty.

Jane clasped Kitty's hand, while Elizabeth said, "It would mean being separated from them, which will be difficult, but with Jane marrying, it would happen in any case."

"I will tell you something, but you must absolutely keep it secret," Jane said. "You must not discuss it where anyone, not even a servant, might overhear." Everyone agreed. "You know that Mr Bingley took only a short lease on Netherfield. He and I have talked about him giving it up as soon as there is an eligible purchase or once the lease is ended. He will seek an estate closer to Pemberley. That would make it much easier for us to see each other."

"I am agreeable," Mary said. "All five of us might not live together, but none of us will be alone if you take my meaning. Not-not yet, at least. I suppose one day, when Kitty, Lydia, or I get married, we will be, but that is in the future. We could not always remain this way. It is not as though we will not see each other."

Elizabeth said, "Not at all. There will be long visits, and we shall be in town at the same time. Even before Lydia, Kitty, and Miss Darcy are out, they can travel with us, if that is their wish."

Lydia grinned. "It depends where you go. Miss Darcy makes Pemberley sound like the most perfect place in England, and while I would like to go to London or Brighton or somewhere like that, if you and Mr Darcy decide to go somewhere boring, I might rather stay behind."

Elizabeth smiled at the girl and rolled her eyes.

Kitty said, "Is it wrong for all of us to-to abandon Mama and Papa?"

Lydia scoffed. "No."

"Lydia!" cried Jane.

Lydia shrugged. "Would you rather I lied?"

Mary said, "I suppose one could say it was abandoning them, but for me, my sisters' well-being is more important. I could not bear it if Lizzy gave up her chance of happiness because of us. You know she would not marry Mr Darcy if it meant leaving us here." Mary closed her eyes and sighed. "Will it not be wonderful to live without the arguments and-and everything else?"

Elizabeth rested a hand on Mary's shoulder, and the five ladies exchanged looks of shared commiseration.

Kitty's eyes watered. She nodded and whispered, "I would like that."

Draping an arm over Kitty's shoulders, Lydia said, "To put it plainly, there is nothing to discuss. Jane will marry Mr Bingley. Mary will stay with them, and with two daughters in the neighbourhood, at least for now, it is not so much like they are losing all of us at once. But Mary, you must promise not to move back to Longbourn, no matter how much Mama tries to convince you."

Mary nodded.

"Papa ignores us all," Lydia went on, "except Lizzy on occasion, and Mama is no example for us to follow." When Jane tried to protest, Lydia said, "I am just saying what all of you are thinking. Mary and Kitty know what I mean. I want to marry a man like Mr Darcy or Mr Bingley. That will never happen if my mother has her way and I end up being empty headed like she is. Everything Lizzy and Jane have taught us about being respectable and what is most important in life—I know I have not always made it easy for you." She gave Elizabeth a small, apologetic smile. "I have wanted to be grown up and enjoy myself instead of learning French or what have you, but you were right." Letting her eyes sweep across all of her sisters, she continued, "I want someone who will love me and take care of me the way Mr Darcy will Lizzy. I want that for all my sisters, not someone like Papa, who cannot even be bothered to check Mama's behaviour so that she does not embarrass us. Jane has Mr Bingley, Lizzy has Mr Darcy, and Mary, Kitty, and I stand a much better chance of finding men like them if we leave Longbourn. When we make advantageous, happy marriages, I will thank Lizzy and Jane, not Mama and Papa."

After such a speech, there was little more to say. Mary reiterated her willingness to live with Jane and Mr Bingley, and Kitty and Lydia agreed with their part of the arrangements. The sisters then spoke about happier matters—dreaming of weddings and spending the summer at Pemberley—until almost three o'clock in the morning.

IT TOOK the better part of a week for Darcy to come to an agreement with Mr and Mrs Bennet, but he did. True to Elizabeth's predictions, Mr Bennet soon lost interest in the subject and told Darcy to arrange matters however he and Elizabeth felt best. Mrs Bennet required more convincing. She said a great deal about Lydia and taking her into society to 'show her off' but seldom mentioned Miss Catherine, which disgusted him. Darcy made some vague statements about being able to delight her neighbours by sharing with them the letters she would receive from Derbyshire and London, telling her about everything Elizabeth and her sisters were doing. He was not entirely surprised when that mollified her objections; she could have glory of bragging about her daughters without the inconveniences associated with their presence. She relented completely after he made a series of promises about visits and arranging for Mr and Mrs Bennet to come to them at Pemberley or London. Darcy believed they would rarely see the Bennets outside of Hertfordshire. Mr Bennet had no love for travel, and Mrs Bennet would claim her nerves could not bear the long hours in a carriage it took to go so far as Derbyshire. She might wish to go to town occasionally, but for some reason, he did not think she would. Sadly, he expected none of the Bennet sisters would miss their parents.

The day after everything was decided, the Miss Bennets spent the morning at Netherfield. Under the watchful eye of Mrs Annesley, they celebrated with tea, punch, cakes, tarts, and all manner of delicious food. Mrs Annesley declared she was delighted that 'two such lively, well-mannered girls' would be joining Miss Darcy at Pemberley, and that she was certain none of them would give her any trouble.

"If we do," Lydia said, "you should immediately tell Lizzy. She knows how to convince even me to do what she wants. I suppose Mr Darcy would be beastly if we misbehaved, though, so I promise to do my very best not to."

Georgiana and the girls had taken to using each other's Christian names, and the Bennet sisters had asked Darcy to do the same. It was easy enough with Jane, Elizabeth, Mary, and Lydia, but he had told Catherine that it would take him time to think of her as 'Kitty'. Privately, she had confided that she liked it when he called her Catherine. The girls said they would try to call him 'Fitzwilliam' or 'Brother', as Georgiana did, but only after the wedding. They had no difficulty calling Bingley 'Charles'. Darcy was not sure what to make of the difference.

After Lydia's statement, Catherine looked at Darcy, her eyes round and alarmed.

He laughed. "Yes, absolutely beastly. Georgiana, tell them how terrifying I can be."

Bingley guffawed. "Only when he is bored, like on a Sunday when he has nothing to do. No need to worry, Kitty. With you and Lydia at Pemberley, to say nothing of Georgiana and Lizzy, my friend will not have the time or energy to be bored. Or beastly!"

Elizabeth, his darling, beautiful soon-to-be wife, smiled. "If my sisters turn my husband into an ogre, I shall send them to you, Charles, and let them disrupt *your* household for a while. I will accept Mary in exchange. She has never given me half as much trouble as a certain someone else has." She wagged a finger at Lydia.

Lydia giggled, threw herself onto the sofa beside Elizabeth, and gave her a loud kiss on the cheek. "But you love me best of all, do you not, Lizzy?"

Her reply was a tickle, which resulted in further merriment when all of the girls save Jane—but including Georgiana, to Darcy's delight—took part in what could best be described as a battle in which tickling was the chief weapon. There appeared to be opposing sides, but he could not determine what they were. Darcy had to stand and move away from the sofa before he was caught up in it. He watched from a safe spot and, as he thought about the years ahead and the joy they would bring, felt bathed in warmth and peace.

I wonder if I ever thanked Bingley for his foresight in renting Netherfield or asking me to visit? I never would have guessed that I would find my happiness here—not only the one woman I could ever imagine marrying but an entire family for myself and Georgiana, with sisters and a brother who also happens to be a dear friend. I will help Bingley find an estate near Pemberley, and when it comes time for the girls to marry, I shall insist their husbands live within an easy distance too.

Without her having to tell him, Darcy knew that Elizabeth's love for her sisters, which would soon include Georgiana, meant that she could not bear to be separated from them for any length of time. He would never dream of interfering with such a marked degree of devotion.

ELIZABETH AND DARCY and Jane and Bingley arranged to marry on the same day at the beginning of March. To Elizabeth's surprise, Mr Bennet seemed to regret the departure of his daughters all at once. The day before the wedding, he called her into his library.

"I do not know what I was thinking to agree to Mr Darcy's plan. Longbourn will be quieter, which is not a bad thing, and my purse will be fuller, also not an evil, but I cannot help but feel I gave up too easily."

She wondered if he were referring to his responsibility to his daughters or if he thought Fitzwilliam would have provided him some sort of compensation if he had withheld his permission a little longer. She decided not to enquire.

He said, "You are certain you wish this, Lizzy? To take on not just a new husband and sister-in-law but also Kitty and Lydia? Girls of that age are troublesome creatures."

"Girls of that age are delightful creatures. I am happy that my marriage will offer them so many advantages."

He quirked an eyebrow. "Is that why you—"

"Of course not!" she cried before he could complete his insulting question. "I accepted Mr Darcy's proposal because he is the best of men. I love him, and I love having my sisters with me. This is what is best for Kitty and Lydia, Papa—what is best for all of us." If he needed her to say it, she would tell him exactly why she would not allow her sisters to remain at Longbourn.

He scratched his cheek. "All of us, you say? I cannot say it is best for your mother and me. She will have no one to talk to or share her many complaints with other than me, and I do not suppose she finds my company any more agreeable than I do hers." He sighed. "Ah, well, I suppose you are right to say it is best for the girls. Without the lot of you requiring new gowns and ribbons and whatnots, I shall have more money for books. *That* is a cheerful thought." To prove his point, he laughed and, in a moment, waved her out of the room.

That afternoon, Jane told her about a lengthy conversation she had had with Mrs Bennet. Their mother had tried to convince Jane that Elizabeth and Fitzwilliam were being very high-handed to take both Kitty and Lydia away. Lydia should stay behind so that she could keep Mrs Bennet company and her mother could take her out into society, 'as a good mother should'. Since Jane would not order Elizabeth to agree, Mrs Bennet next tried to say that Mary should remain at Longbourn.

"I will not tell you what she said about Mary. It was not particularly kind. I told her that Mary did not want to stay," Jane reported. "I said that not only did Mary expect and want to move to Netherfield, but I would also not leave her here because I knew she would be miserable. You look as shocked as Mama did, Lizzy."

Elizabeth was surprised by the vehemence with which Jane spoke. "I am! Good for you, Jane."

Jane blushed. "I was upset, some of it because I knew if I was not...forceful enough, she would harass you about it, and you do not deserve that."

"Neither do you."

Jane waved this away. "I have done what I could for the girls, but we both know that *you* are the one who has borne the heavier weight. Is it wrong that I am already anticipating us moving north to be closer to you? You need not answer; I know you will say it is not. I shall miss seeing you and Kitty and Lydia."

"I shall miss you and Mary, but it will not be for long. Think about how sweet our reunion will be when

Mr Bingley finds an estate near Pemberley. What should be the greatest distance we will accept? Thirty miles of good road? Would it be outrageous to say twenty?"

They shared a laugh before going their separate ways to finish their preparations for the next day.

❦

THE MORNING WAS SUNNY, and Elizabeth awoke feeling lighter and more cheerful than she remembered being since she was a child. The sensation did not dissipate that day or for many more to come. The wedding was everything she could wish it to be. Mary, Kitty, Lydia, and Georgiana were bridesmaids. They had decided that they needed new gowns and that they would be made in the same pink muslin to, as Lydia said, 'symbolise that we are now sisters.'

As soon as the wedding breakfast was finished, Mr and Mrs Darcy and their three youngest sisters began the journey to Derbyshire. Elizabeth struggled to describe her sentiments even to herself. She sat beside Fitzwilliam, their hands clasped beneath a thick wool rug, and smiled as she listened to Georgiana, Kitty, and Lydia chatting like the best friends and sisters they had become. Mrs Annesley was in the second carriage. The girls would travel with her part of the way to give the newlyweds privacy, but both Elizabeth and Fitzwilliam had wanted to start the journey together. Turning her eyes to him, she could hardly believe that she was his wife.

I thought it was impossible. How many times did I tell myself not to indulge in feelings that could only cause me pain? Yet here

I am, here we are—Lydia, Kitty, and me—away from Longbourn and headed to a new life, while Jane and Mary are at Netherfield, their new home.

Elizabeth wished she were alone with Fitzwilliam so that she could kiss him. He had given her so much, more than just his love, which was a precious enough gift. He, and Charles, had given her and her sisters a new life, one in which she would not have to rush them up the stairs to the sanctuary of Jane and Kitty's room or outside to escape hearing her mother and father hurl cruel words at each other or the thumps that spoke of objects, including limbs, being used as weapons.

I suppose what I feel, apart from love and happiness, is relief. But mostly love.

Again, Elizabeth gazed at her husband and allowed herself to revel in the excitement that came with being newly married. She put her mouth close to his ear and whispered, "I love you," at the same time that she tightened her grip on his hand.

His eyes met hers, and the smile he gave her, so soft and tender, made her love him even more. Into her ear, he whispered, "I love you, too, Mrs Darcy."

A loud giggle followed by two quieter ones interrupted their moment.

"We should have taken the other carriage so that they could be by themselves," Lydia teased.

Kitty turned pink, and Georgiana bit her lips together.

Lydia continued, "Once we are at Pemberley, we promise to leave you alone for a week."

With a bark of laughter, Fitzwilliam said, "Be careful what you promise, Lydia. I wager you will not be able to keep that particular one. A week without telling Elizabeth what you have discovered or asking her your customary hundred questions a day? I think not. I will send you all to your bedchambers by seven o'clock, however, with orders that you stay there until morning."

Kitty's alarm was matched by Lydia's giggle. Georgiana assured Kitty that he was teasing: "Which is strange in itself. Before he met Lizzy, I did not know he knew how to tell a joke." The last was evidently meant just for Kitty's ears, but the carriage had fallen quiet as it slowed, and they all heard it.

Fitzwilliam chuckled. "Let us consider it one of the many happy consequences of my marriage. Our lives have changed—all eight of us, including Bingley, Jane, and Mary—and, I trust, for the better."

"Much, much better," Elizabeth said.

The girls agreed, and as the carriage gained speed, putting more distance between them and Longbourn, the new family shared their dreams of what their life together would bring.

EPILOGUE

Nine months later

It was a week before Christmas, and Elizabeth stood at the edge of a pond at Pemberley. Fitzwilliam was beside her as they watched Georgiana, Kitty, and Lydia skate. The sound of their blades on the ice mingled with their laughter. Fitzwilliam would join them in a minute, but Elizabeth, her belly round with child, would not. Lydia and Georgiana were steadying each other, while Kitty skated in circles around them; she was by far the best of them. The sight brought a smile to Elizabeth's lips and tears to her eyes.

I cannot believe how happy we are, she thought. *I certainly am, to have married my darling Fitzwilliam.*

At times, Elizabeth thought she was living in a dream, one in which she and her sisters were enveloped in love and comfort. Always there, his arms seemingly sheltering them, was her beloved husband. He had become her dearest friend. While she and Jane remained on intimate terms, and there was very little she would not tell her older sister, her connexion with Fitzwilliam was different from what she and Jane shared. She supposed it was natural. They were married and saw each other every day, something that was no longer true of her and Jane.

It is not only me. Kitty and Lydia are happy too. I never appreciated how much we were all oppressed by the atmosphere at Longbourn. And soon my sisters and I will all be reunited.

Her heart swelled at the thought, even though it was not the first time they had been together since the double wedding in March.

So much has happened since then, Elizabeth thought as the happy scene before her brought a soft smile to her face.

Her memories drifted back to the day they had first arrived at Pemberley. How delighted she, Kitty, and Lydia had been to see their new home. Despite Fitzwilliam's and Georgiana's attempts to describe it to them, and Elizabeth expecting the estate to be grand, she had been taken aback by its beauty and tranquillity and how quickly it had become a true home. Kitty and Lydia had needed little time settle in, and they were doing remarkably well. Along with Georgiana, the girls had made several friends in the neighbourhood, and, with the help of Mrs Annesley, Elizabeth, and several masters, they were well on their way to being prepared to come out when Lydia was seventeen. Elizabeth, too, had made friends and had grown confident in executing her duties as mistress. Somehow, without her noticing, the months had eased her anxiety. She no longer worried so much about Mary, Kitty, or Lydia, and her relationships with them had become stronger in some ways—more like that of an older sister to a younger one than that of a guardian.

In May, they had gone to town, as had Jane, Charles, and Mary. There, Elizabeth had met Fitzwilliam's family —the earl and countess and their sons—who had been welcoming and helpful as she navigated through her first experience with the *ton*. Lady Catherine, upon learning of Fitzwilliam's engagement to Elizabeth, had sent so disagreeable a letter to him that he had vowed never to see her again until she apologised. Elizabeth's particular favourite amongst her new family was Colonel Fitzwilliam, who was as amiable a gentleman as she had ever met. After half an hour in his company, Elizabeth understood why he was her husband's dearest friend. The colonel was like a brother to Georgiana, and he soon took Lydia and Kitty under his wing, and—when he visited Pemberley that summer—had taught them to ride. Elizabeth had begun riding lessons, too, but had abandoned them when she realised she was increasing.

Before returning to Derbyshire after their time in town, the Darcys, Kitty, and Lydia had gone to stay at Netherfield for a week. It had been the first time any of them had seen Mr and Mrs Bennet since the winter, and, after the first meeting with them, Lydia had said, "I am so very relieved our visit will be a short one. I know you will say it is wrong of me, Lizzy, but seeing them makes me so…angry. I hate feeling that way."

Lydia's confession had led to a meeting of the five Bennet daughters at which Elizabeth had urged Mary and Kitty to also share their sentiments. Kitty had said that she felt as Lydia did, adding, "It also makes me horribly sad. I do not know what I expected, but I thought Mama or Papa might be...well, pleased to see us again. I do not think they care all that much."

Mary had scoffed. "I am sorry you are disappointed, but I am not surprised. My father never had much use for us, and my mother has found ample reason to attend every possible party and make endless calls—she must tell everyone the latest news from Mrs Darcy and all about the splendid life she and her two youngest girls have in Derbyshire—and hardly misses us. Oh, how she boasts about having two daughters so advantageously married and her conviction that Lydia—the daughter that most resembles her—will marry a lord. What does it matter if we are not there to witness her recitations? Everyone hereabouts already knows what we look like. I do think she will miss being able to call on Jane, but her disappointment will be easily assuaged by having more letters to wave under people's noses."

Elizabeth was able to witness the truth of Mary's words during that week. Her mother had insisted on Elizabeth's company while making calls one morning, and they had attended several parties together. As soon as it was apparent that Elizabeth would not crow about her life as Mrs Darcy, Mrs Bennet pushed her aside and proceeded to do the job her daughter had refused to do. They saw Mr Bennet only briefly.

In September, Jane, Mary, and Charles had settled at Oaklands, an estate not five and twenty miles from Pemberley. The trio had spent a month at Pemberley in the summer while Jane and Charles supervised the renovations necessary to make their new home ready for them. During a visit to Oaklands in November, after they had all agreed to spend Yuletide at Pemberley, Elizabeth had raised the notion of inviting Mr and Mrs Bennet to join them. The eight of them had been sitting at the breakfast table, and the silence that greeted her suggestion had lasted two minutes until Jane, her voice tentative, spoke.

"Are you certain that is wise, Lizzy?"

Elizabeth regarded her, then looked at each of her sisters in turn—including Georgiana, who would be asked to share her home with two people Elizabeth knew made her uncomfortable—before her eyes settled on Fitzwilliam. He sat beside her and had her hand clasped in his and resting on his leg. The two of them had discussed the idea previously, and while he did not entirely like it, he had agreed that it would be appropriate. Elizabeth sipped her tea and again let her gaze sweep over her companions.

"I think it is…necessary," Elizabeth had said. "I know that you three"—she nodded at Jane, Mary, and Charles—"have seen them more than the rest of us have this year, but when they agreed to allow Kitty and Lydia to remove to Derbyshire, we assured them they would be asked to visit. Other than those few days we were in Hertfordshire last spring, we have not seen them since March. I will forget the scheme if any of you object. I own, I am reluctant, but…" She shrugged.

Lydia had said, "I do not care if I never see either of them again." When Jane had said her name in reprimand, Lydia had continued, "It is how I feel, whether you think it is right or wrong of me. However, I understand *why* Lizzy has proposed it, and I even agree that it is, as she said, necessary."

Fitzwilliam had smiled at Lydia, whom he was encouraging to think as a responsible adult should, even if that meant acting in a fashion contrary to her desires.

When she had been encouraged to share her opinion, Mary had sighed. "I can bear it for a week or two. Pemberley is large enough that I can avoid my mother if I feel I must."

"You can hide in our parlour," Georgiana had said, referring to the one she, Kitty, and Lydia used as their own.

Kitty had giggled and said, "We shall forget to show it to my mother when she insists on a tour of the house."

Charles had laughed. "That is the spirit!"

The decision made, Elizabeth had written to Mr and Mrs Bennet, making it clear that she wanted Christmas-tide to be full of joy. If they argued, they would be asked to leave.

Now, Christmas was almost upon them. Jane, Mary, and Charles would arrive that afternoon, and Mr and Mrs Bennet were expected the following day. Fitzwilliam had promised to insist her parents leave if they so much as hissed angry words at each other or said or did anything to distress their daughters. She loved him all the more for his reassurances and prayed she had not made a mistake by inviting her parents.

My sisters and I tolerated that life long enough. When we were at Longbourn, we had no choice.

It gave Elizabeth such joy to know that the child now growing within her, and whatever sons and daughters followed in the years ahead, would have the happy childhood she and her sisters had been denied, that her children would have parents who loved and respected each other and them. A part of her would always be angry and sorrowful that her parents had been unwilling or unable to do so much for their daughters. Elizabeth had done what she could to protect her younger sisters from the distress their parents' acrimony and neglect caused. Now that she was the mistress of her own home, she could, and would, do more to shield the girls from Mr and Mrs Bennet's behaviour. What exactly that would entail, she did not know. But, as she had done since she was twelve years old, she would allow her sisterly love to act as her guide.

ACKNOWLEDGMENTS

The title for this novella comes from a poem James Austen wrote about his sister Jane after her death. I was trying to find the perfect title for this story, centred around Elizabeth's devotion to her sisters, and his words about Jane seemed particularly fitting.

My many thanks as always to Amy, Jan, and everyone else at Quills & Quartos for everything they have and continue to do for me. I am very proud to be part of the Q&Q family. My thanks, too, to the authors of Austen Variations, who have offered me a supportive harbour in the online community.

ABOUT THE AUTHOR

Lucy Marin developed a love for reading at a young age and whiled away many hours imagining how stories might continue or what would happen if there was a change in the circumstances faced by the protagonists. After reading her first Austen novel, a lifelong ardent admiration was born. Lucy was introduced to the world of Austen variations after stumbling across one at a used bookstore while on holiday in London. This led to the discovery of the online world of Jane Austen Fan Fiction and, soon after, she picked up her pen and began to transfer the stories in her head to paper.

Lucy lives in Toronto, Canada, surrounded by hundreds of books and a loving family. She teaches environmental studies, loves animals and trees and exploring the world around her.

family into grief as another rejoices in the gift of an unexpected son. Two decades later, a chance meeting leads to the discovery of the lost heir of Pemberley and the man who knew himself as Mr William Lucas is restored to his birthright as Fitzwilliam Darcy of Pemberley.

DISCOVERING THE TRUTH ABOUT HIS PAST means leaving behind everyone and everything he has ever known and loved—including his childhood best friend and soon-to-be betrothed, Elizabeth Bennet. Tormented by questions about himself, and his place, Darcy struggles to understand and adapt to his changed identity and his new life. He must contend with a father buried in the shadows of the past and family relationships he does not understand.

The truth has come out. Some have gained by it, some have lost by it, and I am in the middle. I cannot possibly make everyone happy. No matter what I do, someone will suffer. No matter what I do, I shall suffer.

Somehow, he must find a way to do right by his new and old families, especially if he is to avoid losing Elizabeth forever.

Being Mrs Darcy

One distressing night in Ramsgate, Elizabeth Bennet impulsively offers Georgiana Darcy aid. Scandalous rumours soon surround the ladies and Fitzwilliam Darcy, forcing Elizabeth and Darcy, strangers to each other, to marry.

Darcy despises everything about his marriage to the daughter of an insignificant country gentleman with vulgar relations. Georgiana, humiliated after a near-elopement with George Wickham and full of Darcy pride, hates her new sister. Their family look upon Elizabeth with suspicion and do little to hide their sentiments.

Separated from those who love her, Elizabeth is desperate to prove herself to her new family despite their disdain. Just as she loses all hope, Darcy learns to want her good opinion. He will have to face his prejudices and uncover the depths of Georgiana's misdeeds to earn it, and Elizabeth will have to learn to trust him if she is to ever to find happiness being Mrs Darcy.

Mr Darcy: A Man with a Plan

Fitzwilliam Darcy was a man in despair following his disastrous proposal in Kent. If only he had done this, or said that! If only he had made more of an effort?

Was too late?

Perhaps it was not, for soon after that fateful April day, Darcy unexpectedly sees Elizabeth in London. He seeks her out again, ostensibly to ensure she now thinks better of him. He quickly decides that he wants to win her affections.

It would require effort, perhaps a great effort, but Elizabeth Bennet was worth fighting for.

But in order to do so, he would need a plan.

Made in the USA
Middletown, DE
23 December 2022

20283127R00111